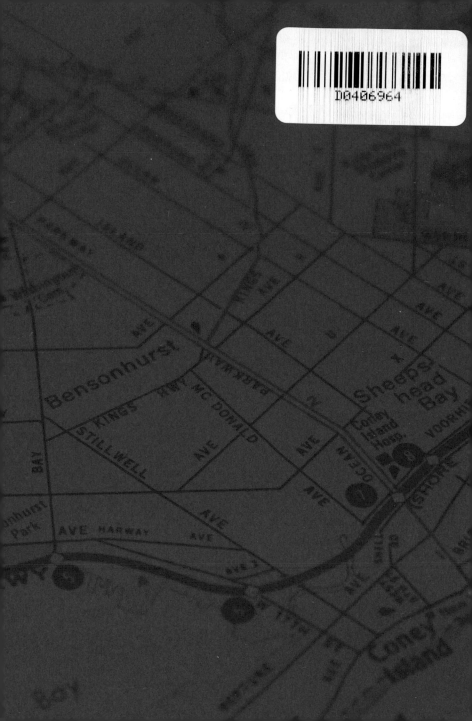

BROOKLYN, BURNING

BROOKLYN, BURNING

STEVE BREZENOFF

carolrhoda LAB

MINNEAPOLIS

Carolrhoda Lab™ is a trademark of Lerner Publishing Group, Inc.

Carolrhoda Lab™
An imprint of Carolrhoda Books
A division of Lerner Publishing Group, Inc.
241 First Avenue North
Minneapolis, MN 55401 U.S.A.

Website address: www.lernerbooks.com

Front cover: © iStockphoto.com/TheCrimsonMonkey. Back cover: © Infocus/Dreamstime.com (left); © Micw/Dreamstime.com (right). Brooklyn map © Alexis Puentes/Dreamstime.com.

Main body text set in Janson Text 11/15.
Typeface provided by Linotype.

Library of Congress Cataloging-in-Publication Data

Brezenoff, Steven.
    Brooklyn, burning / by Steve Brezenoff.
        p.   cm.
    Summary: Sixteen-year-old Kid, who lives on the streets of Brooklyn, loves Felix, a guitarist and junkie who disappears, leaving Kid the prime suspect in an arson investigation, but a year later Scout arrives, giving Kid a second chance to be in a band and find true love.
    ISBN: 978-0-7613-7526-5 (trade hard cover : alk. paper)
    [1. Street children—Fiction. 2. Interpersonal relations—Fiction.
3. Musicians—Fiction. 4. Alcohol—Fiction. 5. Brooklyn (New York, N.Y.)—Fiction.] I. Title.
PZ7.B7576Bro 2011
[Fic]—dc22   2010051447

Manufactured in the United States of America
1 – SB – 7/15/11

For Beth, the "you" in my love story.

—S.B.

"Love is friendship set afire."

—JEREMY TAYLOR

"Here comes Dick, he's wearin' a skirt.
Here comes Jane,
ya know she's sportin' a chain."

—'ANDROGYNOUS,' THE REPLACEMENTS

(THE MURAL)

On the corner of Franklin and India streets in Green-point, Brooklyn, is the north wall of Fish's bar. If you stand across India from Fish's, you get the best view of the mural, twenty feet high and thirty feet wide. It hasn't been there long, and in this part of the neighborhood it doesn't get much attention. Even folks going to Fish's bar don't notice, because they usually walk up from Williamsburg to the south, or along Greenpoint Avenue down from Manhattan Avenue and its bus and subway lines. Those who do see it, stare at it from the launderette across the street instead of watching the clothes go round.

It spans day and night, with the sun rising way to the left—out of a blast of yellows and golds and reds—and the moon and stars blossoming at the right, all indigo and silver and purple and deep, deep black. In between the beginning and the end is our Brooklyn—mine and Felix's—with its blocks and bridges and bottles. Beautiful. Right in the center is the warehouse, looming over the river, stout and ancient. Above it all are our mothers and fathers: the skyscrapers and dazzling glass across the river, holding back while looking down over us, an air of protection (imaginary) and authority (meaningless). And then there's Felix—blink and you'll miss him—walking into the night, with his head low and swinging, and his eyes closed.

On the sidewalk under his loping right foot is written 1986–2005, and beneath that, the signature: KID.

SCOUT

"What about you?"

I asked you that question for the first time on the morning I found you, sitting against the dropped gate of Fish's bar. The sun wasn't even up, and my feet were sore from wandering all night with my bag on my back, looking for nothing but too excited to sleep and unwilling to stay in one place.

You probably don't remember it like I do.

"Are you waiting for Fish?" I said. You didn't even look up from under your dark black bangs, so I kicked your foot gently. "If you're waiting for Fish, she won't be here for like seven hours."

Then you looked up. I didn't notice that your ears stick out, just a little, so you look like a pixie sometimes, or an elf. I didn't notice that the corners of your mouth always seem like they're trying to smile, while the rest of your mouth wants to pout. I didn't notice the little bump on your nose, near the bridge but slightly to the right— the bump I'd trace with my finger over and over, not soon enough. I didn't notice your long hands and rough fingertips, or the dozens—is it hundreds?—of bracelets on your left wrist, made of busted guitar strings.

I noticed your eyes, because they looked wet; maybe it was a trick of the light—the fluorescent and neon lights falling over your face from the bodega next door. But I didn't think about neon or fluorescence, not then. I didn't think about love, and I didn't see right down to your heart. But I must have stared—did I?—because there was your spirit, right there before me, and when you found my eyes I knew I'd pulled that spirit back from someplace amazing, not Greenpoint, not the summer sidewalk in front of Fish's bar, smelling of old alcohol and piss.

But it must have been a trick of the light, because when you stood up, you were smiling, and your bright eyes looked alive and right there, with me, on Franklin Avenue in Brooklyn, New York, Earth.

You didn't answer me, not directly. Instead you reached into the back pocket of your jeans and pulled out a slip of paper and held it out to me. "I'm looking for Felix."

I took the flyer. I'd seen it a hundred times. I was there with Felix when he'd made them. That they were still out in the world . . . It felt like forever ago.

DUO LOOKING FOR MORE. PLAY ANYTHING, BUT BE AMAZING, BECAUSE WE ARE. COME TO FISH'S ON FRANKLIN ANY TIME AND ASK FOR FELIX.

"Felix is gone," I said. I crumpled the flyer to hide the shaking in my hand and tossed it into the street. "If you want to join a band, I'm all that's left of that project."

"What do you do?"

You looked confused, or maybe you didn't believe me. You made me distrust myself, and I looked at my feet, then swung my bag off and pulled out my sticks as evidence. "Drums."

With a little willpower I got my chin to rise and looked at your face. Your eyes were leaving again, going wherever they'd been, so I tried to hold them there. "I can let us in," I said. "If you want."

"Is there a band?"

I noticed for the first time the gig bag leaning against Fish's dropped gate and shrugged. "There can be," I said. "I mean, we can make one. Anyone can make one."

You didn't say anything, just picked up that gig bag, so I dug around in my backpack again and found my key ring to let us into the cellar. When I swung open the gate in the sidewalk, you looked down the steps into the darkness.

"Down there?"

"It's just a practice space," I said, heading down. I found the dangling chain to turn on the naked bulb. "It's nothing fancy. I sleep here most nights."

"I don't think I want to go down there. I don't like being cooped up like that."

I stood at the bottom of the steps, rolling my eyes up at you. "It's barely seven steps down. And hey, we can open the back doors to the garden if you want."

You shouldered your bag and took two steps down, then ducked a little to get a look. It was nothing impressive, of course. I mean, Felix's Christmas lights were still up; if he hadn't come back for three amps and a drum set, he wasn't coming back for Christmas lights. They gave the place a certain charm. I figured I'd plug those in for the full show, and you jumped a little. I admit I laughed.

"Come on," I said, unplugging the lights, then I reached out my hand with a sigh, like you might need help with the steps.

You took my hand and another step. From there I guess you spotted the ratty couch and the back door and windows. They must have made you feel safe. Or maybe I had. I felt your fingers close over my hand, tightly, and then you came all the way down.

"You can put that down if you want to," I said. "What's your name?" I went to the back, toward the garden door.

"Scout." You laid your gig bag down on the couch but didn't sit down yourself. "Can we open that door? For some air?"

I nodded and laughed a little, then opened the heavy bolt and swung the back door open. You followed me as I stepped out into the garden. I sat down on a cast-iron chair, part of Fish's patio set, and lit a cigarette. "The sun's starting to come up," I said, gazing over the buildings behind Fish's place, "from way out at the tip of Long Island. The east end is where the sun comes up. It goes down in New Jersey." That's what Felix told me.

A little panic started rising in my chest, so I took a long drag and exhaled it slowly and coolly into the east.

You sat opposite me, just staring at me for a while. I could feel your eyes on me. When I faced you, you turned and looked at the sunrise. I guess I must have sounded pretty crazy to you just then.

"So, who are you?" you finally said.

"I'm the drummer," I said. "I help out Fish at the bar upstairs when she lets me. I haven't seen my parents in about nine months, but I still go to school for most of the day. Or I did until last week; school's out. I'm also the genius who painted the mural on the side of the bar."

"I saw it," you said. "Where do you live?"

"Right here, like I said. Lately."

"What's your name?"

"Everyone calls me Kid," I said. I don't even look my sixteen years. "As in 'Billy the.'"

"Is your name really Billy?"

"My name is really Kid." I clenched my teeth. "Okay?"

You nodded. "Do you want to play something?"

"Fish would kill us if I started drumming at this hour. Her neighbors are terrible people. They'd have the cops here in no time, and I'm not exactly old enough to be hanging around a bar." I found a scratch in the center of our little patio set and picked at the paint with my chewed-down fingernail. "What about you?"

You looked at my finger as it worked. "Are you asking my age?"

"Why are you here? Where are you from? What's your story?" I prodded.

"It's summer, isn't it?" you asked, and I nodded. "Then it's summer, and none of that matters. For now, I'm whoever I want to be."

I looked up from the table for a minute and into your eyes, saw myself in them, but you seemed to be sliding off again. Your chin went up and your eyes let out for the horizon.

"I need sleep," I said, getting up and stamping out my cigarette in the ashtray on the table. "I've been walking all night just to hit that couch. You've already interrupted my schedule. I should be fifteen minutes into Sleep Town by now."

"Well, do you mind if I plug in?" You jumped up and went in ahead of me. I caught how your jeans sat halfway down your ass, and your long shirt, tucked in, didn't hide how slim you were, almost skinny—hungry. If not for the studded belt holding up those jeans they'd have been around your ankles.

"I'll keep it very low. I can play you to sleep."

I didn't even answer, but you pulled the gig bag off the couch and I took its place. As I closed my eyes and let myself slip away, I heard one of Felix's old amps crackle to life, and then crackle again as you plugged in. You strummed and tuned and strummed again.

The tone was like honey, better than anything Felix had ever gotten out of that amp, and your voice was more delicious still—warm and sweet, but there was a darkness in it, and it showed me all those places I'd seen in your eyes. Your song crept over me as I drifted, the room spinning ever so slightly, and I rolled onto my side and pulled up my knees, facing the back of the couch, and put my hands up together by my chin, like your music was a blanket I could gather around me.

SCHOOL'S OUT

We never talked about where you planned to stay. That first night—I guess it was morning already, really, when I met you—I don't even know if you slept. I woke up still on the couch, but my arm wasn't under my head, going numb pressed against my ear, like usual. Instead your lap was there, and your hand was in my hair, like I was the family dog, and when I rolled onto my back and the side of my face pressed against your belly, your wide-open eyes shined back at me.

I sat up and quickly got on my feet. "What are you doing?"

"Nothing," you said, letting your hands fall onto your thighs. "I wasn't sleepy, so I just sat down and . . ."

I took a step out into the garden, grabbing a cigarette on the way. "Don't get the idea we have some connection now, okay?" I said over my shoulder. "You showed up with a stupid flyer I made a year ago. That doesn't mean you get to pet my head and act all lovey-dovey, okay? It's meaningless."

I lit my cigarette and let the smoke roll between my lips and up my face, up the side of the building, past the fire escapes and along the windows on the second and third floors, over the roof, toward the river.

"Got it," you said, and I heard the amp pop as you switched it on. "No connection. Meaningless."

You started playing, and I told myself the music I remembered as beautiful—ethereal—last night wasn't special. I'd just been tired, riding a little drunkenness. But that was a lie, because I was already feeling my chest about to burst, so I took another desperate drag before pulling the garden door closed and sitting down.

. . .

I burst in through the back door of the bar the moment Fish opened the latch. It wasn't even eleven.

"Is everyone getting an early start this morning?" she said, and I smiled and threw my arms around her neck and wrapped my legs around her hips. She's a goddamn Amazon, and I'm scrawny as hell, so that's no trick. "Nice to see you too."

"School's out!" I shouted next to her ear, then spotted Konny walking toward us through the otherwise empty bar. "Think Jonny'll show up this morning?"

Fish smiled and I released her from my hug to meet Konny halfway.

"I hope so," Fish said. She switched on the jukebox. "I could use the extra income right about now."

Konny and me sat in a booth near the front window and a few moments later a pair of Cokes showed up on the table.

Fish wouldn't ever serve us drinks, of course, outside of Cokes. Coke is fucking delicious, especially on hot summer days like those, and Fish's fountain Coke is the best I've ever had. If you need it flat and fast, it is. But if you're sipping and relaxing for hours at the booth past the stage, it pops and fizzes every time.

"Thanks, Fish."

"Mmhm," she said, and sat down next to Konny. The two of them sitting there could have been related, with their so-black-it's-blue comic-book hair and tattered black leather and lace. "The cellar was wide open when I showed up, Kid. How about that?"

"Oops, sorry," I said. I leaned forward and took a sip from my Coke. "Someone showed up last night—or this morning, I guess—with a flyer, one of the ones we made up last summer."

"Felix's?" Fish asked. Konny turned to look out the window, and I nodded.

"So what happened?"

I shrugged. "Nothing. I came up here to say hi and got sucked in. You know how it is."

"You left a total stranger down there alone?" Fish asked. Konny laughed. "With all that equipment?"

"I don't think Felix will mind," I said, then I took my turn looking out the window. Fish got up and went behind the bar when a couple of hipsters came in, probably looking for Bloody Marys or mimosas or some other morning drink. Konny took advantage to slip a flask from her huge bag and happy up our Cokes a little.

We hung out in the window like that through most of the afternoon. At three, Fish ordered a pie from Danny's pizza place down Manhattan Avenue. When it arrived, Fish paid for it and dropped it on our table. Our jaws must have fallen open.

"You're both going to help out tonight, isn't that right?" she said with a smirk, her hand flat on the top of the pizza box, preventing us from digging right in.

She meant after closing: crating up empties, sweeping up, mopping the bathrooms. Konny and I nodded stupidly and Fish smiled, then let us open the box as she grabbed our empties. "I'll get you two another couple of Cokes."

. . .

My stomach was full and my head was down when someone stepped up to our booth. I saw black jeans and checkered Vans but didn't lift my head. Konny didn't feel tactful; she never does: "Who the fuck are you?"

"I'm Scout."

Your name and voice made my chest sink for an instant, and I lifted my head. "What are you doing here?" I felt like I had to cover you with a sheet, pull you into a closet, lock you away.

You looked at Konny, then back at me. Konny and me get that type of glance a lot, people wondering what we mean to each other, so I rolled my eyes.

"We talked about starting a band," you said, glancing back at Konny. She was busy smirking at me, no doubt wondering if you were mine, and how soon she could get your pants off. The idea of you becoming another notch on her belt bothered me more than it should have.

"Are you around all summer?" Konny said. She slid deeper into the booth to make room for you, but you nodded and didn't sit.

"You want to play, huh?" I said. I got up from the booth and grabbed your wrist. "Let's go, then. See you, Konny."

I pulled you through Fish's place to the back door, past the bar, past the jukebox, past the quarters pool table. Konny shouted after us through a smile, "Awwww!" Two drinkers were leaning just outside the door to the garden, so I shouldered through them, pulling you along, and jerked you down the four steps into the cellar, then went to close the door behind us. I remembered early that morning, your fear of being enclosed, and left it open so you could breathe. Though why you thought breathing Greenpoint's air was any better than breathing in our own steam and CO_2, re-circulating in the basement, was beyond me.

Your old Jazzmaster was hanging from your neck and shoulder before I could even find two sticks unsplintered enough to bother with. The amp thumped into life, then the PA, and the tubes got warm, and then the room did as your music and voice filled it up. I wanted to jump up from Felix's beat-up kit to pull closed that garden door, to keep your song inside the cellar with us, where those smoking and drinking hipsters couldn't hear it.

We were playing, that first time we played, and it already came naturally. You'd start strumming, and you'd look up at me just as you began to sing, not close enough to the mic for your voice to sound full, but near enough so I couldn't see your lips. I only had to listen for a few moments, a measure or two, a phrase, a chorus, one lilt of the melody, and I'd be playing along. It wasn't just the music, either; our bodies' rhythms fell into step together, marched along with your melodies and my beats, and we never fell away, never took a break. Even between songs, the rhythm went on, in my heartbeat and the blinks of your eyes and the tapping of your foot. When you perched on the arm of the couch and laid your guitar on your knee, I put down my sticks and lay down beside you, to just listen and watch. But the rhythm still went on.

. . .

"You know," I said, back behind the kit, as you bent over your gig bag to zip away your guitar, one hand awkwardly on your belt, "you could probably stay here again, if you need a place to stay."

You turned and smiled, and reminded me of myself last summer: eager and afraid. "If it's okay with you, that would be great."

"I'll ask Fish," I said, getting up. You followed me out the back door and quickly into the bar. I stopped short. "Jonny!"

But he wasn't smiling. There was his gorgeous Jonny face and blond cropped hair, with that shock of pink, brighter than I remembered it, right up in front, catching the light from the beer lamp that hung over the pool table. But where was his openmouthed smile? Where were his wide-open arms, inviting me inside?

Instead, his head was shaking, and he was pushing me back, back into the garden, out of the bar. He hardly glanced at you, and something had to be wrong.

"Hold on," came a stern voice from behind him. Jonny's head dropped and he stepped to one side. Two men in pants and jackets—cops—stood with Fish near the front booth. All three were watching me and you. The older one asked, "Is one of you known as 'Kid'?"

I looked at Jonny, but he didn't look back. He just dropped his butt onto the edge of the pool table, then both his palms, like a disappointed teacher on his big wooden desk, and let out a slow sigh.

"I'm Kid," I said, stepping through the door.

"How old are you?" one of the cops said. Who cares which.

I glanced at Jonny, but his eyes were on the tiled floor, so I looked for Fish. She was angry, practically snarling. "Just keep your mouth shut, Kid," she called out to me.

"I'd advise you to keep *your* mouth shut," the cop said, barely glancing at Fish. "If this one's legal, I'm J. Edgar fucking Hoover."

"Come here, Kid," the other cop said, I think. That one might have been smiling, like the "good cop." But there's no such thing as a good cop when you've lived in the warehouse, so who cares, like I said.

Still, I walked over there, keeping my head up best as I could. My bag was over my right shoulder, and I gripped the strap with my left hand, so my forearm cut across my chest.

"I'm sixteen," I said when I reached them. "I told her I was twenty-one. She didn't know I was underage."

"Don't worry about that," the good cop said. "We want to talk to you about the warehouse fire."

"You know about the warehouse fire?" the other cop said. He had a shaved head and sunglasses hanging off his shirt pocket. I looked past them out the front door. Their car was there, double parked.

I nodded quickly. "Yes."

"Kid, don't say anything," Fish said. "Call your parents."

"From what we hear, you don't talk to your parents much. Is that right, Kid?" the bald one asked. They might have both been bald, or close to it.

I shrugged. "Not much, no. So?"

"How long did you live at the warehouse?" one of the cops asked.

I tried to look in his eyes to answer, but mine were getting dry. I blinked a few times. "Not even a year," I finally said. "Maybe ten months."

"Do you smoke, Kid?"

It was the other cop again. Were there three of them? I turned my head, but all the cops were looking at me and I wasn't sure who spoke. My hand went to my pocket, where a soft pack made a rectangular bulge.

"I . . ."

"Where were you on the morning of May second of this year?"

"I don't know."

"You don't know?"

"Do you remember the fire at the warehouse, down off Water Street?" another cop asked. I turned to him. "That fire was in the middle of the night of May first. The very early morning of May second. Where were you?"

I finally let my head drop and looked at the floor. The tiles were cracked where they met the bar. Several stools still hadn't been used that afternoon, with two of their legs still tucked over the foot rail.

I thought back to that morning. The smell of smoke, nothing unusual: it comes and goes with the breeze in Greenpoint. But it was acrid. Burning tires, gasoline. It fell around me like two gloved hands around my throat. It burned my eyes, and left them parched, so I cried without tears, wanting to run and grab Felix by the wrist, to pull him off the couch, take him with me. But of course he was long gone, and I was alone, with cigarette butts and empty bottles of vodka. Wrappers from the Burger King at the corner of Greenpoint and Manhattan. Empty white paper bags from Danny's Pizza. Soon they'd all burn, just so much fuel. I stood for a minute as the smoke billowed around me. The easiest thing would be to take it in. I'd been practicing, hadn't I? All those cigarettes. I was ready for the big leagues. Just breathe it in . . . just breathe it in. . . .

"If you won't talk here, we can take you down to the station," a cop said. I snapped out of my flashback, just a little. "We'll call your parents, the whole deal. Is that what you want?"

"This is over." It was Fish. I felt her hand on my wrist and looked up. An arm fell around my shoulders. "Unless you plan to make an arrest?"

One of the cops smiled. He pulled a phone from his pocket and stepped away from us. The other pulled out his handcuffs.

"Are you serious?" Fish said.

"Put your hands in front of you," the cop said to me, so I did. He put the cuffs on me, more gently than I thought he would.

The other cop came back. He smiled at Fish, then slammed an open hand on the bar three times. "This bar is closed," he shouted, smiling big, like he was making last call, "by order of the New York Police Department. Everyone out, right now."

I looked at Fish, hoping she would look back, hoping she'd forgive me. She'd had plenty of trouble from the police in the short time I'd known her, and this incident would be a point against my presence here, I knew.

"Shit," was all she said.

Jonny came up beside us. "I can be down there in thirty minutes, Kid. If you need bail. I'll come down, just in case. Okay?"

I shook my head. "Don't." I looked back through the bar, at the door to the garden, but you were gone.

One cop took me by the arm, right on my bicep. His grip was hard and I wondered if he knew a special way to inflict pain without leaving a bruise. I assumed he did and tried not to squirm. His partner pushed open the front door and I was led through. It had started to rain, just a little. The raindrops were better spaced than a downpour, and smaller. One of the cops guided me into the backseat and closed the door behind me. There was no cage between me and the front seats, like I would have thought. Soon both front doors opened and closed and the car started. I looked to my right and saw you, standing under the awning of the bodega at the corner—red with that yellow trim, littered with tiny lightbulbs and "grocery," "tropical," "produce," "dairy," covered in years of dirt. Your gig bag hung from your shoulder, against your lanky frame, and in the mist you reminded me of a young soldier, maybe just inside the tree line, with his gun hanging heavily around him, unable to join the battle.

Our eyes met for an instant, I think, and I looked down at my cuffed wrists in my lap, and as we drove away, I hoped they'd lock me up forever.

(THE NIGHT OF THE FIRE)

Monday nights at Fish's bar weren't as dead as you might think, but they weren't exactly a scene either. They were slow enough that Fish would let me and Konny hang out in the back booth. Not that Fish would ever give us a drink, but sometimes she'd look away as one of us pulled a bottle from our bag and sloshed a glug or two into our Cokes—I guess especially since Felix.

Since the beginning of the school year, with both of us sometimes making it to class, Konny and I were pretty inseparable again. I guess with my Felix gone, and with Konny needing a friend who she didn't also screw, it was easy enough for us to forgive each other. That Monday, we'd actually made it to a couple of classes—art and our poetry elective—but after that Konny scammed a fifth of vodka and we thought it made very good company. By the time we reached Fish's place it was after midnight, and we were falling all over each other, laughing or crying or a little of both, loopy and buzzing.

Konny and me mostly leaned on each other, talking too loud and projecting our laughter toward the bar. We stayed that way, the two of us, sipping Cokes and a little something else until Fish decided to lock up early at two. She came to the back and bolted the door to the garden— the smoking section—then leaned across our booth to cart away our empties. "I gotta lock up this shit hole," she said.

Konny and I nodded slowly, more like a gentle long sway of our necks, but we managed to get up. It was the hour when buzzed and tired blend into a very pleasant ride in the womb, and anywhere can be your bed. I swung an arm around Konny's waist and she dropped hers over my shoulder.

"We're a couple of drunks," she whispered, close to my ear, and I laughed.

When we reached the door, it swung open. I hadn't even noticed Fish walking beside us through the bar.

"Where are you sleeping, Kid?" Fish asked as we passed through, into the wee hours.

"The usual, I guess: Felix's old place," I said. "Unless you're going to let me crash in the cellar for once?"

Fish sighed. "I can't, Kid." I glared at her, and the meaning in my eyes was clear: Fish had let Konny sleep down there, but she wouldn't let me.

Fish and I had been through that argument a million times, so don't ask me why I even bothered. "I know," she said off my glare. "But Konny was desperate and was about to get a place of her own. It was two nights!"

I waved her off. Fish was always trying to stop me from staying at the warehouse, at Felix's old place. I don't know her motivation, but she didn't care enough to open her door to me, so it doesn't really matter, does it?

"Same as any other night," I said, and added, "Besides, I gotta walk Konny home," which was ridiculous, because in her three-inch-heeled shit-kicking boots, Konny—with her torn tights and black leather skirt, and her short-cropped raven-black hair—was a very intimidating six feet of femme fatale. Way scarier than I could ever hope to be.

"Why do you *want* to sleep at the warehouse?" Fish said. "Why do you even *want* to sleep in the cellar? Why do you keep surrounding yourself with . . ."

She trailed off, but I knew where she'd been going: with memories of Felix.

I lit a cigarette and said through my teeth, "I'll be fine. I'll be sober by the time I make it back this way, and you'll probably see me again in about ten hours and we can start all over, okay?"

Konny and I waved good-bye as we turned and started along Franklin, toward Williamsburg.

"Or you could go to school tomorrow!" Fish called after us.

I swung my backpack around to the front and dug around for the fifth of vodka, which still had a little left, and we passed it between us while we walked. We didn't say much, just drained the bottle. It ended up smashed against a toilet factory on Banker Street.

Halfway through McCarren Park in Williamsburg, Konny stopped short and I nearly fell.

"What the hell," I said.

Konny nodded toward a nearby bench with a couple of people on it, one of them, from the sound of it, moments from ecstasy. I squinted into the dark but couldn't make out their faces.

"Hey, Ace!" Konny called out, and then I got it. He was in our art class, and Konny and him had been couply for a little bit, maybe a year or so. Ace—dumbest name ever—was one of those Clash boys, always sneering and rolling up the cuffs of his jeans and covering himself in obscure political buttons. Such crap. He had a mohawk— the tall kind—for a year in ninth grade. He was cute, but he knew it a little too well, and got his hands on every piece of ass that would let him. Not that Konny was any better at fidelity.

The ecstasy was averted, and Konny strode toward the bench, heavily throwing her hips: *I might fuck you, I might kill you.*

"Konny," Ace said, feigning pleasure to see her. His benchmate stood and Ace went to grab his wrist, but he took off like a fellating little rabbit.

"Who the fuck was that?" Konny said, and I decided it might be time to make my exit. I wasn't worried about leaving Konny alone with Ace, even though she was drunk and this park was deserted. I might have worried about Ace a little, but I never liked him anyway.

"Good night, Konny."

I crossed back over Bedford, alongside the school, past the tennis courts, and I could still hear Konny's shouting. When I moved onto Banker—down the canyon of factories and underground clubs—Konny's voice switched off, blotted out by the brick and cement blocks.

In my pocket, my thumb ran over the textured wheel of my lighter, over and over, until I remember my breath was a little short and reached for my cigarettes. I'd meant to quit, since Felix, but I hadn't gotten around to it. I suppose I was waiting for a reason.

The wind off the river was shooting down the Banker Street canyon, so I stopped walking and took cover in a doorway to light up; I guess I wasn't as practiced as I thought I was. Finally I got a little of the tip to burn orange and dragged hard. The cigarette started to burn down one side, but finally caught and burned evenly. I let the smoke come in with my breath and sighed it back out. Then I looked out from the doorway down Banker, toward the warehouse. I knew right away I wouldn't be sleeping there that night. I wouldn't be sleeping there ever again. No one would.

. . .

By the time Konny found me, I was sitting on the curb across West Street, near the corner of Meserole, just watching. Fire trucks were already there, and more were on the way. Apartment building doors began to open and the streets began to fill. I felt a hand on my back and then Konny sat beside me and wrapped her arms around me. I shook, and laughed that I had a chill so close to all this heat.

Konny stayed with me, watching the firefighters, watching the warehouse burn from the inside, to a charred husk, for hours. It was long after sunrise and the firefighters were still trying to contain the blaze when Fish came running down West, completely in a panic.

Konny and I watched her approach. "Do you think our parents know where we stay?" Konny said. I looked up at her but didn't reply. Konny's eyes went wet and she looked back at Fish, who was almost upon us. "I wonder if they'd care."

Fish threw her arms around both of us and cried. We all cried, I guess, and she led us up Calyer and along Franklin and said, "You're staying in my cellar as long as you need to," and with people staring we walked in a group hug all the way to her bar.

GREENPOINT TERMINAL WAREHOUSE

I never even made it into a holding cell. Instead I sat in a small, boring room, waiting for my parents to show up. No one said anything. A new cop was there, an older, uglier one. His face must have been made of leather. I wondered if this precinct had a token female and where she was, if she planned to join us.

My father didn't say anything. He sat next to me and bubbled toward boiling. My mother sat on my other side and held on to my arm, comforting but looking for comfort too. She took my chin in her hand and looked at my face. She'd missed me, she said.

Everything was clean and clinical now. There was a tape recorder on the table in front of me, and I answered everything right into its microphone.

"Yes, I have slept at the warehouse.... For about ten months ... summer of 2005 ... That's when I left home."

He didn't even shift in his seat. My mother's hand moved up and down my forearm, once, and she gripped my elbow hard.

"I spent most of that night at Fish's bar.... Yes, the one you found me in, on Franklin.... A couple of blocks from the warehouse, yes ... What do you mean? Oh, yes. I was drunk when I left the bar that night.... A friend, only. I left with her, and I walked with her to, um, McCarren Park. Then I turned around and headed back to Greenpoint, back toward the warehouse.... I don't know. Like I said, I was drunk. It was late. After two, I think...."

He asked me if I smoked when I got back to the warehouse. I said I didn't remember. He asked me if I was still drunk when I got back to the warehouse. I said yes, probably. He asked me if anyone else was at the warehouse. I shrugged and said probably. There were usually people at the warehouse. Lots of people slept there.

"But not in the section where you slept, is that right?"

"There were a few," I said. "It wasn't only me."

"Did you start the fire at the Greenpoint Terminal Warehouse on the morning of May second of this year?"

I looked at the microphone, and then at the tape recorder itself. I didn't say anything.

"Would you like me to repeat the question?"

I shook my head. "I don't have to answer, right?"

"Sweetie . . . ," my mother whispered at me. My father didn't move, didn't breathe.

"You have the right to remain silent," the cop said, repeating from the list of rights he'd given me earlier.

I nodded and sat back in my chair. No one moved for a minute, no one spoke. Finally my father stood up.

"We're finished?" he said.

A cop sighed and I waited. He looked at me. "We've got nothing to hold you on, but we'll want to talk to you again. You're advised not to leave town." He handed me a business card. It said he was Detective Tye Blank. "I'd also advise you to stay with your parents for a while. I don't want to involve social services."

My mother and I stood and followed my father from the room and down the hall. We went past the front desk and out the big double doors, down the front stone steps, past ten cops in uniform, smoking, and turned east to walk along Meserole, across McGuinness, to our home. Dad opened the door to our building, and then the door to our apartment. My mother and I followed him in. When the door closed with a thud and click, he said, "Did you start that fire?"

I looked at him, then hitched my bag higher onto my shoulder and walked into the bathroom and locked the door. A shower would be nice.

. . .

I got dressed in my room, then repacked my bag with some clean clothes and went through the living room. I couldn't stay in the apartment, not when I knew Fish was closed down, that Jonny was finally back, that you were out there too, maybe with no place to stay. I went for the door, but my father moved quickly to block it.

"Not yet," he said. "First, answer my question. Did you start that fire?"

"What difference does it make?" I said. "Who cares about that stupid warehouse? Even if I did burn it down, I'd have been doing the neighborhood a favor. It was a blight. It was disgusting. It had no value. It needed to come down."

"You're not leaving this apartment, not tonight," my father said. He looked over my shoulder at my mother. She was sitting on the couch in the living room. The TV was on, the volume up enough to drown us out. She didn't look at me or my father; she just looked at the TV.

"Dad, you kicked me out of this apartment, remember?" I said.

"And you went and became an urchin and burned down the warehouse. So now you're staying put."

"So now I'm not allowed to leave? Make up your mind!"

My father crossed his arms and leaned against the door. "As soon as you make up your mind, we'll make up ours."

I squinted at him, working it through. "What's that supposed to mean?"

"I think you know."

"Move."

"Did you burn down the warehouse?"

I hitched up my bag and stepped toward him. "Yes. Move."

He stepped to one side, opening the door for me as he did.

My mother got up from the couch, but she didn't say anything and she didn't make a move to stop me, so I went through, out of the apartment.

BY ORDER OF THE NYPD

It's a long walk back to the river, and it was already after ten. I don't know what I hoped to find there; with Fish's place closed, Jonny wouldn't be around, and you . . . I had no idea what you'd be up to. I probably should have found Konny. Instead I headed west.

The first full day of summer was nearly over. During morning rush hour and evening rush hour, you'd never know summer had begun. But at this time of night, there was an obvious shift. The streets were filled with people, like always, but these people were different. These were high schoolers, out late, buzzing with freedom as much as anything else. These were people like you; people who took their freedom a little farther, and found Brooklyn. People like Jonny, who appeared every June and vanished every September, and no one asked why.

There were college kids too, renting for the summer while they interned three hours a week at some publisher or nonprofit. Maybe they nannied on the Upper East Side. When they moved in groups up and down Bedford, I could quickly size them up and make a good guess: Vassar, Sarah Lawrence, Barnard? Purchase, NYU, Oberlin? Each was like a species of bird, and if you knew which had a crown of red feathers or a green streak along its back or a belly of speckled gold, you knew them through and through.

I walked along McGuinness as long as I could. I didn't want to see any people, but cars I didn't mind so much. They flew down the boulevard, mostly north, into Queens, probably to the 59th Street Bridge, to Manhattan. A few streamed over the Pulaski toward me as I walked. Finally I hit Greenpoint Avenue and turned left, down toward the river. There were pedestrians immediately, walking three or four wide down the sidewalk. I stepped into the street and walked between parked cars and traffic. I crossed Manhattan and descended to Franklin.

"Kid!" It was Jonny, sitting at an outdoor table at the Pencil Factory, the bar on the corner. The table was full of empty glasses of various sizes, and I knew he was the last remaining at what must have been a full table. I wondered when the next shift of Jonny admirers would arrive, and decided maybe that it was me.

Jonny got up, finally smiling, and opened his arms to me, so I fell into them. I'd missed his hugs, so I let it go a little longer than I knew I would next time. He ran a hand up and down my back, in that way he does that makes me wonder where the line between lust and love is, between appropriate and not, and I pulled away and sat down in the empty seat across from him. I smiled up at him.

"Hi, Jonny," I said. "I'm glad to see you."

"I'll get you a drink. Sit tight." He went off to the bar and I watched him weave through the heavy wooden tables inside, to the people standing at the bar. He leaned over them, pushed into them, always smiling, and being smiled at. It didn't take long for him to get the drinks. Both must have been buybacks, since he never paid for them. Soon he was back at the table. He put a tall skinny glass, a vodka cranberry with a slice of lime, in front of me. I slipped my lips over the red stirrer and took a long pull on it. It was cold, and I shuddered, but I liked it.

Jonny looked at me. I ran a hand through my hair and then a finger up the side of my glass. "Jonny," I said. "This summer is fucked."

He laughed and nodded. "Not what I expected first day back. I hadn't even heard about the fire." He leaned forward. "Was it you?"

I lifted my eyebrows and took another long sip of my drink. "It doesn't matter," I said. "I'm just worried about Fish. Do you think they'll keep her closed?"

Jonny shrugged and lifted his glass. "I doubt it, not for more than a couple of weeks."

"A couple of weeks?" I said, sagging. That's an eternity on summer time. I pushed the stirrer aside and took another sip. An ice cube slid up and tapped the tip of my nose. "Do you know what happened to Scout?"

"Scout?" Jonny said. "I don't—Is that the new guitarist you were dragging around today?"

I nodded.

"Cute," Jonny said, leering a little.

"All right, cool off," I said, smiling. I blushed a little.

"Anyway, I have no idea," Jonny said. "What about you? Do you have anywhere to stay?"

"I guess I'm back home," I said. I finished my drink, and then used the stirrer to suck up the last watery sip. "I mean, for now. The cops threatened to put me in foster care, pretty much."

"Ooh, ouch," Jonny said. "Social workers."

I laughed in spite of myself and stirred the ice in my empty glass, then pulled out the stirrer and started chewing it. My soft pack was in my back pocket, so I reached for it, but when I stuck my finger in and groped to the corners, I found it was empty.

A big man came up to our table. He was head-to-toe in denim. His round, chinless face was well bearded. He was wearing John Lennon glasses and holding a pipe. He smiled at Jonny, who got up from the table, and I got up too with a few of Jonny's cigarettes and lit one, then slid the rest into my own pack. "Bye, Jonny. I'll be around."

Jonny smiled at me and waved before he threw his arms into a new, extra-large hug for the next visitor, and I walked away feeling lonely. I'd meant to go home after that drink, but the last place I wanted to head was home, lonely as I was.

Instead I headed two blocks out of my way, to Fish's place. I just wanted to see the door, to see if they'd posted one of those notices from the NYPD. They had, and I stood there like an idiot reading this stupid six-word notice on its caution-orange paper, glued crooked and wrinkled right on the heavy metal outer door, behind the dropped gate: "Closed by Order of the NYPD."

You came up next to me and read it too. I didn't even turn, not at first. The truth is I wanted to turn to you, so close to me, shoulder to shoulder as we were, and put my arms around your neck. "I thought I'd never see you again," I wanted to say, panting at your ear, but I didn't.

"I didn't expect to find you here," I said instead.

Out of the corner of my eye, I saw you shrug. "I've been wandering around here since you . . . left," you said. You shuffled a little and pushed back your bangs. "I was looking at that mural. It's really good."

I coughed and let a finger slip into my pocket to play with my cigarettes. "Thanks."

"Who's the boy?" you asked.

"That's the boy on your flyer," I said. "That's Felix, off into the sunset."

You didn't say anything, and a car thumped along Franklin behind us, its speakers booming Dominican beats.

"I guess you still need somewhere to stay, huh?" I said.

"Seems like maybe you do too," you replied.

I let myself turn to face you, and took a step back. Your eyes were right there with me, not shooting off on some interplanetary voyage. "I'm going home," I said. "It's late. You can come, sneak in. They won't even know we were there."

"Who?"

"My parents," I said. "Come on." And I took your hand, just for an instant, to turn you around to follow me. When I let your hand fall again, as we started walking, you used it to hitch up your gig bag, and I slid mine into my pocket for my lighter.

(THE FIRST TIME
I HEARD FELIX)

Are you ready to hear about Felix? I contrived to meet him on the first day of summer break that year, 2005. I was meandering in Greenpoint, kicking around with Konny like we did—before Konny was working down at the comic shop.

"What should we do?" Konny said.

It was hot. The air was thick with the smell of roasting garbage sitting in black bags on the edges of the sidewalks. We were stopped at the little ice cream window on Greenpoint Avenue, and Konny was working on her cone. I didn't feel like ice cream, but I was considering dropping a couple of bucks on street meat: something on a wooden skewer with a hunk of bread, but the man at the corner of Manhattan Avenue wasn't in his usual spot.

I kicked at the iron rail Konny was leaning on, then grabbed it and leaned way over, till the sharp little accents running along its top, like spearheads but shaped like tiny pineapples, poked me in the belly. "Anything," I said. "Anything we want for three months."

"It stinks," Konny said. "Let's beat feet out of here, anyway."

"Yup." We headed down Greenpoint toward the water. As we crossed Manhattan, we heard a strum on a thick-toned guitar. "Is that a Telecaster?"

Konny shrugged. "Might be an SG. It's muddy as hell." Konny was the only guitarist I knew then. We played around a lot, mostly down at the high school so I could use the school's kit in the music room. We weren't a band exactly; Konny wasn't interested in getting good or playing anything beautiful. Not like Felix, and not like you. She just liked to play loud and she'd often turn to me while we played and spit on me, then laugh. This was the year she took my clippers to the back of her head. "Boy in the back, girl in the front," she'd said.

"Let's go see." We rounded Franklin and stood at the corner for a minute, trying to pinpoint the source. Konny thought straight, closer to the warehouses down on the water, where every cool kid with a black-and-white *film* camera shot nearly every picture in their senior portfolio for art class. I'm not a photographer, though. I'm a painter.

"I think it's down here," I said, thumbing north.

The right answer came from an unfamiliar voice. "It's under Fish's bar." A youngish—but old enough to drink at noon, I guess—skinny guy with white-blond hair was sitting at a table outside the Pencil Factory, the bar on the corner where we were standing. Konny and I turned and faced him, Konny all sneers and squints, me all apprehension and longing. He was drinking a tall red drink, nearly empty, with about ten chunks of lime squashed in it. Across from him was an empty short glass with a cigarette butt in it. Oddly, he was smiling, sitting there alone, watching us. It was Jonny, of course—Jonny who smiled at me from our very first moment.

"Where's Fish's bar?" Konny asked. Jonny pointed over our heads, and Konny turned to look. I kept my eyes on Jonny, though. "I don't see any bar." Konny turned back, sneering more deeply.

Jonny got up, leaving his drained drink and his invisible tablemate, and walked over to and past us. He crossed Greenpoint and got about ten steps farther down Franklin before stopping and dramatically turning to us, arms akimbo. "Coming?"

I smiled and ran at him, then waved Konny to come along too. With a roll of her eyes, she did.

"What are your names? Mine's Jonny."

"I'm Konny with a 'K,' this is Kid."

"Also with a 'K,'" I added.

"Konny. I like that: you come right after me." Jonny danced his eyebrows, then led us across Kent and Java streets. "And here's Fish's place. Easy to miss, huh?"

Its front was just a door off the street and two big windows, one with a Pabst sign, switched off. The windows were too dirty, and the inside was too dark, to see anything at all. But there was no doubt: the gorgeous guitar was coming from the open cellar doors at our feet.

"And down there is Felix."

Jonny went into Fish's place, and Konny gave me a look: *Should we go in?* But I wasn't interested, because that's when Felix began to sing.

I don't remember what he sang about; I'm not sure I ever knew. It was his voice, gritty but gentle, like my father's hands when I was too small to see past them, and the slow way his melody moved along its path, not in any hurry but enjoying every note for itself, rather than looking forward to the next note, and the next, until the song's end. This song would have no end; it couldn't possibly. This song was forever.

That's what I thought. And I knew right then, letting Konny take my hand and pull me into Fish's place for the first time, that I'd meet the person with that voice.

TAKE THE BED

"I guess I thought you had run away," you said as we walked along McGuinness. There was plenty of traffic on the boulevard still. The BQE, over and in front of us, was stopped dead, like usual, as it approached the Queens border.

"Not exactly," I said. "I was evicted."

"Your parents kicked you out?"

I nodded and glanced left and right quickly. You looked back and forth too—but nervously, with your lip tucked in and under your top teeth. When the traffic cleared enough, I muttered, "Come on," and then jogged across the boulevard, knowing you'd follow my lead. You did.

"Tonight my father wouldn't let me leave, though," I added when you reached me. "I'm trying to figure out how to get in without anyone knowing, especially how to get you in." I laughed. "They'd love that, meeting you."

You looked at your sneakers so I shut up and quit laughing.

"It's on the next block." Ahead, across from my building, an SUV was parked with its windows open and music blaring. All we could make out was a fast beat; the bass shook the whole car. If I hadn't seen and heard this scene a hundred times before, I might have thought the back window would blow out. On and around the stoop of the building closest to the car, about ten guys hung out, screaming to each other and drinking beers.

"We're across from the party. They might be awake." I let us into our building and led you up the two flights to our apartment door. "Let me check first. Don't move."

I opened the door and stepped inside, leaving the entryway light off. The apartment was silent, so I stuck my head back out the door and grabbed your wrist, hissing at you: "Okay. Come on."

I couldn't let your wrist go, not this time. I let my hand slide down a little, to your open palm, and felt it close over me. We went down the cracked linoleum floor of the hallway, hitting every creaking spot. I wasn't worried; my parents usually sleep with the window open, but that night, with the party going on at the stoop across the street, I knew my father would have insisted on the window air conditioner being on in their bedroom. It would drown us out.

My bedroom door stood open. My dirty, street-lived clothes lay in a pile on the carpet. I closed the door and locked it when you came in, finally letting go of your hand. I didn't turn on the light.

"You can have the bed," I said, watching you in the dark. Enough light came in through my venetian blinds, dropped to the floor and sealed up tight, so I could make out your slim figure. I watched you look around and find a place your guitar might be safe. You leaned it in the corner and knocked my little trashcan over. It was empty.

"Leave it," I said. "It doesn't matter. Just be quiet."

"Sorry," you whispered back, moving toward me. "You take the bed. I don't mind. You probably miss it."

"Okay." I pulled one of the two pillows off my bed and dropped it on the floor, then followed it with a blanket. "If you need it. It's pretty hot, I guess."

"It's fine."

I turned away from you and faced the window, then opened my buckle. I kicked off my shoes, then sat on the edge of the bed and pushed my jeans down and over my knees to the floor. I got under the cover quickly and said good night, but I watched you in the low light, looking around again, sitting on the edge of my bed, pulling off your sneakers, standing again, opening your jeans and letting them fall around your ankles, stepping out of thcm, stretching out on the floor, pulling the blanket over you, up to your chest, staring at the ceiling, probably wondering what the hell you were doing here.

(HOW I ENDED UP ON THE STREET)

"So, I got a job," Konny said one morning in July, last summer.

She didn't really have a choice. I never heard details, but for a couple of days she'd been hauling her duffel around a lot and I was pretty sure she wasn't going home. "At that comic place on Metropolitan. For Zeph."

I nodded. Me and Konny were sitting on the loading dock of one of the old warehouses off West Street. Under us, the pavement was losing its fight against the weeds: nature was storming the beach at Greenpoint.

"Where are you sleeping?"

I looked over at Konny, sort of sideways, squinting a little at the sun just peeking out from around Quay Street. She'd pulled up her cutoff cargos and was picking at a scab on her knee. Then she looked out at the river, or maybe out at Manhattan, and twisted up her mouth.

"Zeph says I can sleep on the futon in his office until I find my own place."

"He gave you the job and a place to stay? Wow."

Konny went back to her knee, pressing on the bloody spot with her thumb, then pulling it away until the flow picked up again, then putting it back and pressing again. "He gets a lot of indie fans in there, and I guess I blew his mind with my vast expertise on the world of independent comic publishing. Plus, you know, I've given him my god-damn allowance since I was about five. He owes me." She looked at me and smiled and I weakly smiled back.

"Where have you been sleeping, though? I mean, meanwhile—you haven't been home in a few days, right?"

Konny shook her head once. The cropped section of hair had grown in a little bit, kind of funny and uneven. "Fish let me sleep in her cellar."

My chest got tight and warm. "With Felix?"

"I haven't seen him much, actually," Konny said. "He just practices there. And sometimes he passes out on the floor. But he must have someplace else he usually stays."

Konny and I had been hanging out at Fish's a lot, mostly before the real night scene would get going. We got to see a few of Felix's sets, and Fish was always there working, and Jonny was usually there hanging around. But I hadn't thought Fish and Konny had gotten close or anything.

"Why did Fish let you stay?"

"I asked her to let me stay," Konny said. She licked her thumb and shrugged. "I guess I was kind of a mess—crying and . . . and shit."

She chuckled, and I knew she didn't want me looking at her, so I pulled my eyes away and onto the river. It was fairly still that morning. Konny took my hand, and it occurred to me that I had no idea what day it was.

Konny and me were never more physical than that. Neither of us wanted to be, though I tried one time. We were leaning on each other in the alley behind her parents' place, and Konny was thumbing through an issue of *Fables*. She looked down at me when she laughed sometimes, so I'd ask her what was funny and she could read me a panel or page.

I let my hand slide up from her knee, along her thigh. Konny closed her comic and moved it away.

"What are you doing?" she asked, so I faced her and threw one leg across her lap, then lowered my face to her long throat and kissed her collarbone. She pushed me off.

"What the hell?" I said.

"Are you serious?" she asked, laughing.

I got up and walked across the alley and kicked the cement wall. One of those stencils of Andre the Giant looked at me.

"Isn't that what you want?" I said.

"From you?" Konny said, and it stung, so I walked away fast. Konny wasn't letting it go, though. She followed me on her long legs and had a hand on my shoulder in ten steps. "Come on."

"Am I so bad?" I asked without turning around.

"You're not bad at all," Konny said. "I love you. I love you because you're not bad. You're my . . ."

I looked at my feet. "I thought it's what you wanted," I said. "It's . . . it's always what you want. All those boys and girls that follow you around."

"Is that all?" Konny said. I felt her arms close around me and her chin on the top of my head. "You're just doing what you think you're supposed to do?"

I shrugged against her and she laughed.

"Be the one I don't have to do that with, Kid, okay?" Konny said, and I nodded. And that was that.

. . .

Konny headed to work after dropping me at Fish's. She had to run down and grab her bag from the cellar, so I went down there with her. The only lights on were a few strings of flashing Christmas lights, hanging across the low ceiling and along the pipes on the right wall. Felix— a skinny boy with dark short hair, in torn cargo shorts and a beater—was sitting on the grimy yellow couch, strumming an unplugged electric guitar, eyes closed, and humming.

"Hi, Felix," Konny said. She grabbed her duffel. "Bye, Felix." Then she smiled at me and headed up the stairs again. I just stood, watching him, listening to the melody he hummed. Even without words, it haunted me—it filled the room and everything in it. The visions it gave me: they were dark, but beautiful. They took me out of the cellar, up to rooftops at night on the lower East Side, down into the subway, onto the tracks, and into the tunnels. They brought me deep into the city, deeper than anyone can ever really go: into its heart.

I stared at him, willed him to open his eyes and see me, but he never did.

Back upstairs, the early afternoon sun was too bright, so I joined Jonny at the bar.

. . .

Dad packed my bag for me. Just before the sun came up some morning that August, the bag was sitting on my bed, waiting for me when I came in. I stood there, staring at it, swaying a little on my tired feet and a beautiful rocking wave of vodka.

A light clicked on in the corridor behind me, but I didn't turn around.

"You're drunk."

I nodded, looking at the duffel and at the collage of models I'd made when I was nine, all now with their eyes blacked or gouged out with a ballpoint pen. The collage was surrounded by my sketches—still lifes and nudes and abstract shapes and curves I could remember shading for hours, focusing all my energy on the tiniest square inch of the page—and looking from one sketch to the other I could trace my growth as an artist. I could see where my stroke had changed, had suddenly improved.

"Where did you drink tonight?"

I didn't answer. Didn't turn around.

"Who were you with? Konny?"

I slipped my hands into the pockets of my baggy jeans and lifted my elbows in a lazy shrug that didn't end. The truth was I had hardly seen Konny in the last few weeks. She was spending all her time at the comic shop or working out with Ace, and I was always at or under Fish's place.

"I know her parents threw her out. If that's how you want to live too, then here's your chance." He sniffed and cleared his throat. "That's everything you deserve to take. Don't be here when we wake up."

A moment later the hall light clicked off. I took my bag and twenty dollars from the grocery money in the kitchen and went back to Fish's place.

. . .

The gate was already down, and Fish already home in her bed. If I'd known where to find her, or where to find Jonny, I might have. If the cellar was open, I'd have happily slept down there. But instead I stood in front of the dropped gate, holding my bag, thinking I'd stay awake and on my feet until Fish showed up to open again for the day drinkers. In a neighborhood like this one, with writers and musicians and artists in every loft, Fish got a lot of day drinkers.

While I stood there, though, drifting off on my feet, wishing for a little more vodka and thinking of finding

Jonny to get some, the cellar doors flew up and open. The rust-colored panels slammed into the cement of the sidewalk, one just inches from where I stood. My reverie was shattered.

"What are you doing here?" Felix's head stuck out from the cellar steps. His deep-set eyes were half closed—as open as I'd ever seen them—and his dark, short hair was pressed flat on one side, like he'd been sleeping.

"Nothing," I said. I looked down at my ratty sneakers, already looking like a street kid's, and spoke into my chest. "I'm just waiting for Fish to open."

Felix clambered out and swung the cellar shut, then locked it. "She's not going to be around for hours, kid."

I lifted my head and stared at him, startled at his tone. "I know. I don't have anywhere else to go, so I'm going to wait."

He was a little shorter than me, and skinny. His mouth was small and his lips seemed to purse slightly, now and then, in a rhythm. I wondered what music was in his head.

"You can come with me."

"I thought you slept in the cellar," I said. "Where are you going?"

Felix started to head across desolate Franklin, and I took a quick step or two so I could shuffle beside him. "Sometimes I sleep down there, but Fish doesn't like me to," he said. "Have you been to the warehouse?"

"Of course." Everyone I knew went down to the warehouse; it had always been like that, probably since right after it quit being in the business of housing wares.

Felix loped. His long neck put his head out and down, so it seemed to dangle before his shoulders, rather than on them. He had the gait of a hungry hyena.

"I saw your set tonight," I said. Felix and I still hadn't played together; he didn't even know I was a drummer yet, though it seemed I dropped hints at every opportunity. I looked at my feet and the long shadow I was casting as the sun came up behind us. "Last night, I guess, since it's morning now."

Felix pulled out a cigarette and offered one to me, so I took it. He lit it for me when we reached the opposite corner. "Did you enjoy it?" he asked, and the lighter flickered and bloomed at the front of his cigarette as he spoke.

"I thought it was amazing." We kept walking, on toward Water Street and the warehouse complex. The sun on my back had warmed my neck a little and I pulled off my backpack and let it hang from my free hand. "I love your voice. You know that." *You must, the way I swoon when you play.*

Felix might have shrugged, but he stopped and didn't face me, just closed his eyes. I wondered how old he was. He could have been thirteen, might have been thirty.

"I don't know my own voice," he said, then took a long drag. "When I'm singing, I'm somewhere else completely. The songs are a mystery to me when I'm not inside them." He opened his eyes slightly, just for a moment, and saw me. "Do you know what I mean?"

I fingered my cigarette and followed him when he began to walk again. "I guess I do. When I play drums, I get lost in the music sometimes. But the way you describe it sounds much deeper."

He nodded as he walked. I couldn't be sure whether it meant yes, or simply was an effect of the mechanics of his walk. "Why don't you have anywhere to stay? What happened?"

"My father asked me to leave."

Felix smirked, and for an instant I felt tiny, tinier than I was, tinier than Felix, and I waited for his wisdom. We turned on Water Street and cut across it toward an entrance to the warehouse complex. "So you've got your freedom," he said. "The question is: what will you spend it on?"

I followed Felix through the weeds and rubble, up some decaying cement steps, and into an old loading dock. That's as far as I'd normally have gone, with Konny or anyone from the neighborhood, to just sit and drink. But Felix kept walking.

He led me through a big open room, with beams lying diagonally from ceiling to floor, walls of pocked cement, the reinforcement bars visible through scars— left by vandals or time, no difference. Light snuck in through the dirty cracked windows, where the green paint they'd been covered with had peeled away, or where whole panes had been smashed. The light hung in the room in dusty pockets, and every step Felix took among the rubble sent a new cloud of tiny fragments of cement into the stale air.

For me, it was like imposing on an ancient city, where people once worked and lived. I imagined the men—in my mind, all stocky and crew-cutted, in heavy cotton shirts, dark green, with sleeves rolled up to their biceps. They smoked on the job, and managed to laugh now and then in their somber way, though the work was hard and the only air in the room came through the huge fan blowing smelly air in, off the East River. At lunch, they'd take their metal lunchboxes down the access road through the warehouse complex, and maybe sit where they could see the skyline. Over the years, they'd seen the buildings of downtown get higher and higher, and then midtown. They'd watched the Twin Towers grow, and though empty, the warehouse still stood after the towers had fallen.

Felix took me up a flight of stairs—I was surprised by how stable they seemed—then another, and we came to a door standing open and went through. Some rusty cots were piled in the corner, and a couch and an old kettle grill were in the middle of the room. In the far wall was a tall narrow doorway with an arched top. It led out to a fire escape.

Felix went over to the door and looked out for a moment. He pulled out a cigarette and said. "Isn't it amazing up here?"

After a drag, he moved to the couch and sat, and I walked past him to the fire escape and leaned on the door frame. It looked out over the access roads of the complex, and beyond that I could see the waterfront buildup—

condos and condos—down in Williamsburg. I heard Felix flick a cigarette lighter, and I pulled out my own and a cigarette and lit one for myself. Turning, I saw Felix hunched over on the couch. I knew right away he was shooting up, and I don't know why it surprised me, since I should have known. He was never really "there."

I turned back to the outside and wondered how soon he might fall asleep so I could leave.

. . .

I got back to Fish's bar before noon, but she and Jonny were already inside, flirting across the bar at each other while Fish got ready for the small but reliable crew of daytime drinkers, Jonny himself first and foremost. When I walked in, they both jumped a little; even Jonny's smile looked flat, just for a second.

"Hi," I said, just as flat.

Jonny recovered and gathered me up in his hug, while Fish slapped open the register and filled it with change for the day.

"What are you doing here, Kid?" Jonny said.

"I haven't seen Felix yet today," Fish added without looking at me, but answering the question she thought I'd come to ask. I shot her the stink eye and climbed onto the stool next to Jonny. "Coke?"

"Thanks," I said. Jonny put a firm hand on my thigh so I'd know he was on my team, and because he liked having a hand on my thigh. I didn't mind. "Fish, I need a place to stay."

I felt Jonny's cringe through his hand. Fish looked up with a sigh and put down the glass of Coke. It was already sweating. I wrapped both my hands around it, cold and wet, and leaned forward to take the straw into my mouth. I looked down the length of the straw at the surface of the soda and ice, popping and fizzing onto my cheeks.

"I was thinking maybe the cellar," I went on before Fish could say anything, before she could start explaining, kindly, how insane this was. "It would just be until I find someplace else, like with Konny."

"What happened at home?" Jonny asked. He turned on the stool and faced me.

I shrugged. "I came home drunk, and I guess my dad heard about Konny being evicted, which is ridiculous. I mean, she got kicked out for always bringing fuck buddies by, right? For screwing Ace all over her parents' apartment. In the kitchen, for Christ's sake. Wherever he said 'go.'" I pulled another sip up the straw. "I never brought anyone home. So what if I have a few drinks in the summer?"

I knew what it was about, though, really. Jonny and Fish did too, from the little glance they exchanged. I made Dad uncomfortable, virgin or not—just like Konny made her folks uncomfortable. Bringing Ace home, girls home . . . whoever—what difference did that make? Konny liked to fuck; kicking her out just said "not here;" it didn't say "not at all." As for me, who knows—maybe it would have helped if I brought someone home so my parents would be able to put me in a box, a check mark on a census form.

The Coke was about drained, so I sucked at the diluted remains, then stirred the ice cubes around and around the bottom of the glass. "Plus, yeah, my dad's a bigoted asshole, I suppose."

I looked up at them both, at Fish and Jonny, because I knew how much bigoted assholes made them angry, indignant, and defensive of yours truly. Jonny gave Fish the look he uses when I just want one goddamn vodka and cranberry, but Fish's face stayed stern and she pulled away my empty glass to refill.

As she placed the new Coke in front of me, she said she was sorry.

"You let Konny," I said.

"Konny was a mistake," Fish said, a little regret in her voice. "I could have been arrested. I could have lost everything."

"I don't have anywhere else to go!" I said, throwing my hands up. I let them both fall back to bar. They made a loud slap, and my hands stung.

"Come on, Kid," Jonny said. "We'll find somewhere for you to stay."

"No, I know what this is about," I said, glaring at Fish. "There's no reason you should have let Konny stay but you won't let me. It's because you don't want me hanging out with Felix."

Fish laughed quickly. "Like that wouldn't be a sensible reason all by itself."

I slapped the bar again and stared her down.

Fish wasn't having it. "He's a goddamn junkie, Kid!"

Jonny jumped up from his stool. "Hey, hey," he said, ever smiling. He put a hand on mine. "Stay with me tonight," Jonny said, trying to take me off the stool, but I shook him off. "Come sit at the back booth with me, Kid. Cool off a little."

"It's illegal," Fish said, really leaning into me. "I can't let some—Christ, Kid, how old are you, anyway? Sixteen? Not even?"

I could hardly believe she didn't know. "What does that matter? You'd rather I was living on the street?"

"I'd *rather* you went home and worked it out. I'd *rather* that I stayed out of jail and kept my bar so I can at least get to see you—and Konny and Felix and Jonny and the people I *love*—before you all start fading out and blowing up and disappearing on me." Fish's fist came down hard on the bar. "Shit."

She grabbed up her bar towel and jammed it into her back pocket as she walked away, toward the end of the bar and past the pinball machine, out of sight.

Jonny's arm was around me, and I let him lead me off the stool. I picked up my bag.

"Let's clear out a little while," he said.

It was even hotter outside. We strolled easy toward Greenpoint Avenue, and Jonny deposited me on a chair among the tables outside the Pencil Factory. "I'll get us each a drink."

I sat and looked into the bar, where Jonny was standing, with one foot on the golden rail, leaning over the waxed wood and giving some other bartender his two-thousand-megawatt smile, then down Franklin toward West and the old warehouses.

"You've got a new roommate, Felix," I said under my breath. Then a vodka and cranberry with three wedges of lime landed in front of me, and Jonny sat down.

. . .

Jonny eventually bought me four more drinks and a grilled cheese. Looking at him over the last drink, wiping some butter onto the thighs of my jeans, I said, "Thanks. You don't have to do all this for me."

Jonny waved me off and pretended to blush.

"I'm serious," I said. "I mean, I have a little money, and I can get by. Besides, I'm going to have to learn to, right? You can't support me forever."

He shrugged. "If you needed me to, I would."

I just shook my head and slurped at my drink. I was already pretty drunk. "Why do you have such an easy life, Jonny? You never seem to work. You just hang out, buying drinks and drinking drinks and getting phone numbers of the prettiest people. What gives?"

I knew about Jonny, really. And Jonny knew I knew. But no one ever said it out loud, at least not around me. Even Konny never said it aloud, and she'd call out a priest in church if he looked at her funny. Maybe the vodka made me finally say something—finally challenge Jonny to tell me to my face. Maybe I hoped it wasn't even true. But for that apartment and hundreds of free drinks and adoring looks in every bar in Brooklyn, there was no other explanation. Jonny's assets were his smile and his body.

Instead of accepting my challenge, Jonny laughed and stood up, then grabbed my empty plate and a couple of empty glasses. When he came back to the table, I was gone, west on Greenpoint, my duffel bag bouncing against my thigh and the slippery residue of grilled cheese on my lips.

. . .

I should have paid closer attention when Felix was leading me through the warehouse that morning. Blame it on my condition and the distraction of going anywhere with Felix. His entrance was easy to find, because Konny and I had sat there, dangling our feet off the docking bay, smoking cigarettes and passing a bottle back and forth, dozens of times. But once I climbed up and inside, the daylight was gone, and the few rays of sun that snuck in through the cracks and holes in the roof just disoriented me even more.

I tightened my grip on my bag and stepped over some chunks of concrete and rebar. There was a broken window mostly covered with a beat-up sheet of pressed wood in front of an iron grating; it looked familiar. I went toward it and peeked through a splintery hole out over the river.

There were steps to my left, and I knew Felix had led me upstairs, so I took them. They were cracked and crumbling in places, and up the left side was a railing of old pipe and repurposed two-by-fours. As I climbed, my head began to swim, with alcohol a little and with the climb itself, longer than I remembered it being with Felix. I knew I'd gone the wrong way.

The steps ended in a wide-open room, piled full with garbage: old mattresses, a couple of empty barrels, hundreds of empty clear bottles, even the removable seat from a van. It wasn't garbage, of course. It was someone else's home, not Felix's, and I'd wandered in. I stood there a moment, holding the makeshift banister, letting my spinning world slow down, come to a stop. The room was cluttered, full almost to the cement ceiling in places, with junk—old rusted barrels, like the kind that sit in the alleys on Northern Boulevard, between Quick Lubes and dealerships; some old box springs and two thin, stained mattresses, piled together; rags, piled together in corners and under a broken coffee table, with just two legs on the same end, so it sat like a long right triangle. But the stench hit me hardest.

I pulled my sleeve across my lip, under my nose, and sniffed. It reeked of gasoline and of piss and alcohol. The whole warehouse had those smells, but in here it was overwhelming. I thought the inside of my nose might singe and bubble into flames. Then something crashed to the floor at my feet and I jumped. Near my feet the shattered remains of a clear glass jug spread into shards and dust. Quickly, I turned and headed back for the steps, but someone grabbed my arm. I pulled it away and ran, taking the steps two at a time, until I slipped and took the last few steps on my ass.

I got to my feet and faced him. He was old and bald, and bent at the waist so his shoulders hunched a little. He looked fat, but it might have been layers of clothing.

"Don't ever come up here," he shouted at me in a heavy Polish accent. I started to turn away, then quickly covered my face with my arms as another empty jug flew at me. It bounced off my elbow and smashed against the wall, shattering. "Fat little toddler! Don't ever come up here!" I grabbed my arm and backed away, picking up my bag. The pain flew up to my shoulder like a shock. I hoped nothing was broken; it would definitely bruise.

I turned and spotted another set of stairs across the floor. Felix was coming quickly down as I reached them. "Holy shit," I said, and I threw myself against him.

"Yeah, you shouldn't go up those steps," he said, almost laughing. His eyes were dark and deep, and mostly closed. "That guy's bananas. 'Don't ever come up here!'" he added, aping the man up the other stairs. "I think that's all the English he knows. It's definitely all he ever says."

"He called me a toddler."

Felix stood and looked at me, more than he ever had before. "You have a young face."

I let him lead me up and up to his little room with a view. I collapsed onto the couch. "Fish won't let me sleep in the cellar."

Felix shrugged. "I'm not surprised. Me and her, we fight about it all the time. That's why I usually sleep here."

"She let Konny, though," I said. Even I was getting sick of that argument.

Felix dropped onto the couch next to me and patted his lap, so I slid over and rested my head on his thigh. "So you'll stay here," he said. "I have plenty of room, and the rent is really reasonable."

I forced a little smile and looked up at him, but he wasn't looking at me—he was fiddling around in the pocket of his hoodie, I figured jonesing. He came out with just a couple of cigarettes, though, and slid one between my lips.

I said thanks between my teeth and let him light it for me, then curled up on my side. My bag was on the floor in front of the couch, and as Felix let his fingers run through my hair—absentmindedly, not really there—I realized I'd moved in.

. . .

I woke up alone. For a moment I was confused; the light was dim now, and nothing looked familiar. Then I remembered the couch I was on, and the view over the access road behind me off the little cast-iron balcony. Then I remembered the Polish man down one set of stairs and up another.

I hissed into the dark, "Felix." Nothing moved. I grabbed my bag and moved slowly out of the room. When I found the steps, I ran down, into a deeper darkness, then spotted light around a corner and went to it. As I hit the doorway, I nearly fell off the loading dock, but stopped just short and hopped down.

It wasn't as late as I'd thought. The sun wasn't even all the way down behind me and the warehouse; inside, on the first floor, it had seemed like the middle of the night. I figured Felix was up at Fish's, and Jonny would be too. Besides, it wasn't like I had any other place to go: I couldn't stay with Konny. I mean, she probably would have let me, but did I want to sleep on the floor of her little studio behind the comic shop, while she and Ace worked their way through the Kama Sutra on the twin futon across the room? No, thanks.

Valentino gave me a very smooth and gliding high five as I walked in, with a little smileless nod—Valentino's not much of a smiler. Fish's door guy was a tall man, always dressed like Joey Ramone with a dash of Prince, and up on his stool he towered over me. He always felt something like pride to me, like a lion, with his neat dreads and long face.

Fish hardly looked up from behind the bar as I walked in, but she did shake her head thoroughly and push the air in front of her like it was me. Jonny sat on his stool in front of her, surrounded by plenty of drinkers vying for Fish's attention. He jumped up and grabbed my elbow when I turned to walk back out.

"Kid, wait," he said. He glanced over his shoulder at Fish and said in my ear, "Head downstairs and hang out a few minutes. I'll talk to Fish, okay?"

I tried to say okay, but my mouth was dry, so it came like a click of phlegm with a hot breath on each side. Jonny pulled me deeper into the bar, through the crowd in the front and past the pool table out the back door. The cellar door stood open, and Felix's Christmas lights flashed inside.

"Just give me five minutes," Jonny said. He winked and gave me a solid slap on the rear to urge me down the steps into the cellar.

Felix wasn't there. He might have been up in the bar, with how quickly Jonny pulled me through there. The place was a swimming mass of hot bodies, and I'd just kept my head down and let Jonny pull me through. My parents could have been humping on the pinball machine and I probably wouldn't have seen them.

I found some sticks in fairly good shape, on the floor near the tom, and sat on the throne. I wasn't really feeling like a beat, so I just closed the snare and let the sticks fall onto the skin, very gently, letting them bounce and barely adding to their momentum—just enough so they'd stay on rhythm. When the roll was nice and tight, I let the volume go up, and up. My eyes closed, and the snare swelled, totally under my control. At my whim, the roll suddenly snapped, then dropped back down to a soft, long hiss.

But Jonny didn't need five minutes; at least, I don't think it could have been that long. When I opened my eyes, Fish was standing in front of the set. I pulled up on the drum roll.

"Hi."

"Sweetie, I'm sorry." Fish smiled at me. She looked out of practice.

"Does that mean I can sleep down here?" I asked. I laid the sticks across the floor tom and then flicked open the snare. It rang for a second, until I put my palm over its skin.

Fish's smile became a bit tighter. I jumped up from the stool and headed for the door.

"Wait a second!" Fish said, moving to block the door. I didn't look her in the face. Instead I looked at her hair—cropped short, dark blue. I looked at her cocky stance, her black boots, planted apart. Her legs were tree trunks. "Kid, you have to understand, I can't let a sixteen-year-old kid sleep in the basement of my bar. I will go to jail."

I started to say "Konny," but she cut me off. "Konny was a mistake. Honestly, if I'd known then how young she is . . . I can't believe I still let you two hang out upstairs."

I looked at my sneakers, eternally damp and covered in grunge, and slid my fists into the pockets of my jeans, feeling barely my fifteen years—Fish didn't need to know I was still four months shy of even Konny's age.

I felt her hand on my shoulder and cringed a little. "You know," she said, her voice calm now and soft, "you could go home."

"And what?" I snapped, twisting myself to get her hand off me. "Ask for forgiveness? Fake it until I can move out for real, or until I'm done with college, or maybe I can wait till my father is dead and hasn't been driven to write me out of the will because I've managed not to offend his fucking sexual sensibilities for fifty years?"

"Kid, I—," Fish started, but I wasn't done.

"Is that what you did, Fish? Did you wear a pretty prom dress in 1995? Did you smile just right for the boys so your folks would let you stick around?"

She didn't have anything to say to that, so I grabbed my bag off the cement floor and stomped past her, out into the garden.

"Wait," she called after me. "I want to help. Somehow."

I stopped at the steps and turned around. "How are you going to help? Want to talk to my dad for me, teach him about 'live and let live'? Maybe sing 'My Conviction' for my mom? She'd get a real kick out of it."

Fish looked at me, and I felt bad for an instant. She wasn't my enemy; she wasn't my mom or my dad. She was just like me, in a lot of ways.

"You need money, right?" she said, reaching into her pocket of tips. "You have to eat."

"I'm not going to take your money, Fish," I said. "Come on."

She thought for a moment. "Go upstairs and sit with Jonny. I'll keep you sweet with Cokes all night, okay? Then help me clean up a bit, and I'll pay you."

"Are you giving me a job?"

She shrugged and managed to smile, but I think she was crying a little too. "No vacation time, and no health benefits. And I can't match 401K contributions. But some cash, all the Coke you can drink, and unlimited use of this cellar . . . to practice, not sleep."

I took a deep breath and let myself smile back. "Okay."

When Fish opened her arms at me, I ran into them and forgave her.

. . .

The night was long, but fun. Jonny spiked a couple of my Cokes, and we laughed at the poseurs and at Konny and Ace when they showed up and drunkenly made out against the pool table, sending four dollars worth of spot-saving quarters all over the sticky floor. Cleaning up with Fish was fun too, since she let Jonny and Konny stay to goof around while I mopped and carried empties around. It was almost five when Fish finally locked up. Felix hadn't shown all night.

The worst part of the night came after Ace took off. He and Konny had just finished one of their fights that usually proved to be foreplay, but this time Ace was drunk enough that he just stormed out of Fish's to walk back to Konny's apartment. She fell into the back booth next to me, and I squeezed a little tighter up against Jonny's side.

"Fuck," Konny said. She dropped her head to the table with a thud. "Ow."

Jonny elbowed me, so I put an arm around Konny's shoulder. "Wanna stay with me and Felix tonight?" I asked.

Konny rolled her head back and forth twice to say no, then suddenly lifted her head. "Fish is letting you stay in the cellar?" she asked, stunned.

"No, down at the warehouse," I said.

Konny shook her head again and laughed.

"What?" I said. Jonny reached out his free hand for his drink and took a long, loud sip of melted ice, barely tinted the red of his vodka cranberry.

"I can't believe you're staying at the warehouse, that's all," Konny said. "Your dad finally kick you out?"

"Your sympathy is overwhelming," I said, and I ran my finger through the puddle of condensation next to Jonny's glass.

Konny shrugged. "What do you expect? Since Felix showed up, I've hardly seen you. Maybe if you would hang out sometimes we'd share a place or something. Someplace, you know, safe and clean and free of junkies."

"Right, it's me," I said. "Like I'd be able to pull you out from under that asshole Ace anyway."

Konny laughed again and got up. "Okay, Kid," she said without looking at me. "I'll see you in school in September. Later."

And she walked out. Konny and I had fights before—respectable ones that didn't lead to screwing and we always worked it out. Konny's hot-blooded, I guess, and sometimes when her hot blood mixes with my icy veins, it storms.

Jonny gave me a squeeze, but I was okay and told him so. He smiled back, and for the first time ever I saw it in his mouth but nowhere else on his face.

. . .

"Where are you heading?" Fish asked me after the gate fell with a clank, probably waking the poor suckers who had to live above her bar. Jonny was already gone, to his apartment across McGuinness, and Konny was by then back at her little studio, where Ace had already slept off his drinks and was probably up for her by the time she showed up.

"To Felix's place," I said without turning around.

"The goddamn warehouse?" Fish said, like it was huge surprise, and she moved to stop me, but I hopped backwards with a smile—not totally sincere—and started away quickly while Fish fumbled with her heavy padlock. Soon I was walking fast toward Calyer and Quay, and hoping Felix would show up to stay with me soon.

. . .

Felix never invited me to play with him. He acknowledged my drumming now and then with a soft smile or a hard glance—if I fell in the pocket just right, or hit a nice on-the-one, or if I wasn't dropping back into halftime just how he wanted me to—but mostly I just filled in some space for him. I didn't mind; jamming with Felix was the most reliable way for me to hear his songs and his voice.

Still, we'd become a band somehow, just by virtue of my showing up. We played every day, every night—usually more than once. We'd stop for food sometimes, and plenty to smoke out in the garden. Sometimes we even crashed on the couch, or on the grass in the back garden, despite Fish's rules; she never knew. And I guess I didn't see Konny a whole lot, then. Her prediction of missing me until September looked about ready to come true. Not that it was entirely my fault. She barely made it to this side of the BQE, between work, her place behind the store, and giving it up to Ace whenever he asked.

Felix and I were walking along West Street early one morning, before the sun was up, before Fish had even locked up the bar. Felix let his key ring spin around his finger as he walked, and said, "We should get more people."

I glanced at him through a squint as some smoke came out of my nose and floated up my face. "For what?"

"The band," he said. "We should get a bass. Keys, horns . . . hell, a goddamn orchestra." He stopped and looked down Quay at the warehouse and over the river. "French horns."

"You're Brian Wilson."

He laughed a little. "Why not? He had the right idea. Bigger and higher and greatness. Way past the horizon."

We walked down Quay, through the open gate in the tall chain-link fence, and across the weedy old parking lot, all the way to the retaining wall of broke-down cement slabs. We sat down and each lit a new cigarette.

"Are you serious?" I asked. "About the band, I mean. I kind of thought you didn't much care."

"Of course I care," Felix said. "It's all I care about."

I looked out over the river. "You never say anything about it. You just play. You never even say, you know, 'That was good,' or anything."

Felix took a deep drag and let it out, then shook with a chill as the wind came up off the river. "I think we've gotten good, you and me. And I think if we take it one step further, one level higher..."

"One step beyond!" I said, smiling, glad for Felix's positive mood, but suddenly his voice dropped away and he closed his eyes.

"I can't stay here, Kid."

I dropped my cigarette and stepped it out. "I know."

We stood together, and I wanted to put my arms around his spare frame, hold his head against my chest. But instead I said, "You're leaving Brooklyn, Felix?"

He blew gently through pursed lips, in a long, thin sigh. "It's not Brooklyn. I love Brooklyn. But yeah, I guess I am."

I'd never heard Felix say so much, and I struggled for words to reply, but he went on. "I also hate it. Three stories, one lot, a square block, rows upon rows of square blocks, rows upon rows of three-story buildings—just brick walls around fenced-off gardens, tiny hidden sanctuaries, filled with little patio sets and self-standing hammocks and hipsters with ironic beers."

I nodded. "Where you gonna go?"

He might have shrugged, very softly. "Where can I go? A different city? A different country?"

"You could." *We* could.

Neither of us said anything for a few minutes. When I reached into my pocket for another cigarette, I bumped Felix with my elbow, and he suddenly smiled, snapped from his reverie. "Let's make flyers, Kid. Let's get more players. Let's really do something."

His excitement was so contagious, so rare. I hopped on my toes a little. "Okay. Let's do it."

"Right now."

"Yeah, right now! Fish has a copier in her office upstairs."

Felix threw an arm around my shoulders and I leaned my head against his, and together, in that half hug, we walked back up Quay to Fish's place.

. . .

Nights and days at Fish's blurred together as that summer tumbled to its end. Jonny would get me alcohol, at his place or from his pocket or at the bar down the street. And sometimes, when Fish was in a good mood, a sly wink from Jonny would land me a nice vodka and cranberry juice, just like Jonny's, and the two of us would huddle in our back booth, where we could easily sneak out for a cigarette by the back fence, or just sit and watch Felix on the stage. Fish was giving him more and more sets, just him and his guitar and voice. Not with me, of course. She wouldn't let a fifteen-year-old punk like me near the stage: an underage customer on display for the world? Nuh-uh.

When I was full of drink and watching Felix, my eyes would glaze over, and I'd think about how beautiful he was—his heart and his face and his music—and Jonny would let me lean on his shoulder.

"You're smashed for this boy, huh?"

I nodded against him and let myself smile. It didn't happen a lot. Not then.

Jonny shook his head slowly and picked up his drink. It was sweating.

The bar was nearly empty, and Felix's voice floated softly between the cracked linoleum of the floor and the punched tin on the ceiling. When the last song was over, he sat quietly on his chair, like always, lost. Fish strode up to me and Jonny and started in, wiping the table right under my nose.

"Let me just get this drool," she said. I kicked her in the shin. "Ow."

Jonny smiled and nudged my shoulder so I'd get up. "Smoke."

The three of us went outside. Fish glanced at the bar. Two regulars sat there, drinks well topped off. The bar-back, Gino, leaned against the rack, with no empties to collect and no stock to replace. It was very slow.

Jonny lit our cigarettes and then his own. "You should be careful, Kid."

I looked at him, hard. I was very drunk, since his nod-and-wink routine was working like a charm on Fish that night, and I'd had quite a few drinks.

"I'm fine," I said. "It's not like I have far to go."

The two of them looked at me. What the fuck was this?

"You gave me the drinks!" I snapped. "I've been drinking all summer, since you knew me. It's always you, Jonny. You're the one helping me get fucked up, helping me to forget that it's really just summer and I'm really just lost."

Fish sighed. "Sweetie . . ."

"It's true," I said, softly now. "I don't want to remember that summers end, that I won't be going home, back to normal—that I'm really . . . just a street kid."

Jonny put an arm around me and I went on after a breath. "I'm safe with Felix, anyway. Everyone loves Felix."

"Everyone does," Fish admitted. "You do more than most, sweetie."

My head spun. What was this about? Drinking—or Felix?

"Just don't get too close, Kid," Jonny said.

"He's a mess." Fish took a hard last drag and dropped her cigarette, then stomped it out. "I love him, and I've known him a few years, but he's not sticking around. Something's going to take him from you."

Jonny's smile slipped, just for a second, and he looked at Fish. "She means he wanders, Kid," Jonny said. He squeezed my shoulders harder, affectionately. "It's the kind of soul he's got." I felt him shrug. "Fish and me, you can count on us to be here, whenever you need us—me in the summer, anyway. That's why, you know, a drinkie drink now and then is not a big deal. But in a month or a week, in a minute, Felix could be gone."

"He's not a mess," I said, looking squarely into Fish's green eyes. "Is this just about the heroin?"

"'Just'?" Fish said. She laughed and went back inside.

"Sorry, Kid," Jonny said. "We worry about you, you know that. We worry about Felix too, but, well . . ."

"'Well' what? He's beyond help?"

Jonny shrugged again, and I flung my cigarette butt at the back fence, then went down to the cellar. Felix was already there, laid out on the couch. His guitar leaned on an amp, crackling gently. I switched it off.

"Why'd you do that?" Felix muttered.

"I thought you were asleep." He shook his head, and I walked over to the couch. "You want it back on?"

He shook his head again, so I sat on the arm and ran my hand across his head, front to back, then again, and he reached up and took my hand. I leaned down and found his mouth with mine, gently, our lips barely meeting because we were not close enough. I had to strain a little, to get closer, and he pulled me down, so our mouths pressed together. I turned and slid down off the arm so I was next to him, and he wrapped himself around me.

And then I knew Fish and Jonny were right. I was smashed for this boy, but it was too late.

WE GO UP

I slept on edge, with you on my floor and my parents a door away, so I was awake at dawn. I leaned across to the blinds and pulled them apart to see the sickly orange of a Greenpoint sunrise, so gorgeous at its source but made grotesque by the air between Brooklyn and the end of the island.

It was Monday morning, I realized, and I could smell the coffee and hear the gurgling of Mom's ancient percolator. They'd be getting ready for work: my dad packing fish at the factory a couple of blocks away, and my mother working as a nurse at Maimonides, the hospital in Boro Park. Getting out of the house would be tougher than getting in. I swung my legs off the bed and found my jeans. Then I kicked your foot.

"Wake up."

You rolled onto your side and pulled up your knees for a moment. I heard you suck in a deep breath, and then you stretched your long legs down, pointed your toes and nearly purred like a cat in the sun. With your eyes still closed, you smiled then twisted onto your back. You faced me as your eyes opened and I caught my breath.

"Hi."

"My parents are awake. We'll have to be quiet and go out the window."

"What kind of trouble are you in?"

"Didn't you hear?"

"I heard something about a fire, but . . ."

"Another time." I smiled at you and found your jeans. "Get your pants on." I tossed them over your face.

. . .

The fire escape off my bedroom is over the back garden. With your gig bag on your shoulder, you stood next to me and leaned against the wrought-iron railing, looked out over the backyards of my Greenpoint block. Like most of Brooklyn, our collective backyards were more like the central courtyard of some medieval fortress: no alley to reach them, no entrance of any kind without going through someone's house.

Every little yard, barely twenty feet wide, was closed in with a ten-foot-high fence. Ours was typical: mostly cement, with a sad attempt at landscaping along the fence. A collection of old paving stones was piled in the corner, where our back fence met our side fence. At the house behind ours, they'd built a little patio and installed a hot tub. To the right of us, they'd let it go wild. They didn't go back there, not ever. My dad used to smoke in our backyard, but he quit smoking when I was a baby.

"We can't get out that way," I said, putting a hand on your arm. "Obviously."

You looked out still, then around you.

"We go up," I said, and it was clear you weren't from the city.

The chipping old paint of the narrow-runged ladder up to the third floor stuck into my palms and fingers as I climbed. My shoulder bag, heavy with some fresh clothes and more art supplies, tried to pull me off the ladder. At my upstairs neighbor's fire escape, quiet, I stopped a moment to look back for you, then I went on, up the funny straight ladder to the roof, that U-turned at the top, bent over the ledge. I stopped at the top and looked down after you, then out at the sunrise.

"Too bad we can't linger a little," you said, coming up next to me. "It's pretty."

I shrugged. "I heard once that Greenpoint has the most colorful sunsets and sunrises in the city, 'cause of all that pollution. The chemicals in the air make for better colors."

"Really?" you said, looking at me sideways. "That's depressing."

"I guess."

We lingered after all, just for a minute.

"I like the sunrises back home," you said, more quietly now, like our moment of silence had set the precedent and your voice might disturb us.

"Where's home?" I should have asked.

"Never mind," you said, and you took my wrist. "We're going down the front, right?"

Then you let me go and turned away, strutted across the cooled tar roof toward the black pool ladder at the front.

"Be careful, okay?" I called after, then I followed.

We'd been walking in silence for a block or two when you spoke up. "Can you hang out today?"

I slipped my hands into my pockets and pushed them down till my elbows were straight and my jeans gathered a little at the ankles. "Sure. If you want to."

"I'd love to play again."

"The bar's closed. I don't know for how long. We should probably stay out of the cellar too."

"Right."

I led you under the expressway, past the McDonald's. I could smell sausage, between gasps of urine and exhaust, and it made me hungry. "We can find Konny. She'll be opening in a little while."

"Is Konny . . . are you two, you know, together?"

I rolled my eyes and sucked my teeth, but didn't answer.

We walked quietly for a few blocks. I kept my eyes ahead and tried not to try to let my hand brush yours. When it did, you hitched your gig bag and looked around you, like Jon Voight in one of the movies you made me watch, on his first day in the city or something. My stomach growled and I grabbed it, but you couldn't have heard it.

"I have a little money," you said when we reached the strip along Metropolitan Avenue. "I'm hungry if you are. Anything cheap, and I'll buy."

There was a Korean deli open, so we went in and I ordered myself an egg sandwich.

"I'll have the same thing," you said. I watched you from the deli counter as you strode the wide aisles and picked things up from the refrigerated case: blue cheese; a green basket of fresh tofu, three chunks; Red Bull. You looked them each over, then put them back. Finally you chose a plum from the display in the center of the store and brought it to the counter. The wife of the man making our breakfast was standing there.

"Just a plum?"

"And the two sandwiches."

She called to her husband, who was wrapping our sandwiches, and he called back. Then she punched the register and announced, "Six fifty."

You whistled through a smile and pulled out a wallet. I could see into it, just a little, but there were papers and ticket stubs, sticking out here and there, a history in scraps, and for an instant I itched to know where you were from. The husband held out a paper bag and I took it.

. . .

We found a little park—tiny; part of the Green Streets initiative, maybe—and sat on a bench, took up the whole thing, with the deli bag between us and your gig bag leaning on the end. The sandwiches had cooled a bit by then, wrapped only in waxed paper and that brown paper bag. The cheese on the edges wasn't oozing anymore, and before I even took a bite from the sandwich, I scraped with a fingernail at the congealed cheese on the paper.

"Thanks," I said, with my fingertip in my teeth.

"Least I could do."

"What are you doing here?" I asked. "I know, I'm not supposed to ask. You don't have to answer."

You looked straight out into the street. The morning had really begun by then. Traffic was heavy and slow and the smell of Monday morning garbage in the summer was strong. Not the best place to eat breakfast, but at least we were still free.

"I just wanted to see what it was like, I guess."

"Brooklyn?"

You shrugged. "Brooklyn, I guess. I'd never been here before, can you believe it? Manhattan, sure. Even Queens, when I was little and my dad used to slap a Mets hat on my head." You laughed and took another, last bite of that sandwich. Then you wiped your mouth and pulled that plum from the paper bag between us. "But I think I wasn't just looking for a place, you know?"

I finished my sandwich too and found a napkin in the bag. The sidewalks were full of commuters, all types of dress, from suits to sloppy. Most of their ears were covered or filled with headphones, and most of them carried a bag. I looked at my feet, at my beat-up backpack, torn and patched and discolored, and I wondered what these people needed to bring with them, every day, on that subway ride into Manhattan. And I thought I'd risk it, and said, "Looking for me?"

I laughed quickly to cover, but you didn't.

"Maybe. So far I like it here."

I let my smile fade and leaned back, and I wished that paper bag, full now of our empty wrappers and sitting between us on our bench, would just blow away.

AFTER BEING IN A FIRE

"Will you tell me about the fire?" We were leaning on the gate at Zeph's comic shop, waiting for Konny to wake up and open. She was still staying in the apartment in the back, the room that was supposed to be the Zeph's office.

"There's nothing really to tell," I said, hugging my knees. "This old warehouse down on Water Street—right on the river, I mean—it burned for like three days, back in May. No one knows how it started. They're sure it wasn't an accident, though."

"And the cops think you did it?"

I let go of my knees and drummed on my thighs, then dug around in my backpack, hoping I had a few of Jonny's cigarettes left. I did, and I lit one.

"Were you there when it burned?" you asked, like on the edge of your seat.

"Yes. I was inside for some of it."

"Did you start it? Are the cops right?" I didn't answer right away. "I wouldn't care if you said yes, you know. It doesn't matter."

I took a long drag and let it out. "You wouldn't? Not even a little?" I hadn't meant to make you feel stupid, but it came out bratty.

You got up and played with the links in the gate so it rattled and bumped my back. "I can't believe you'd keep smoking," you said, "after being in a fire," and I let my head fall back into the gate so it rattled again.

I held the cigarette between my thumb and pointer and watched it burn. "I know. I only still smoke because Felix did, I think."

"The guy who made the flyer?"

I dropped the cigarette between my knees and squashed it with the heel of my sneaker. "Yeah." I got up. "Let's go."

"I thought we were waiting for Konny."

I pulled on my bag and handed you your guitar. "Let's go to Fish's. We can play in the cellar. I have the key. She'll never know."

MELODY IS WHAT COUNTED

It was probably around noon when we reached Fish's cellar. I unlocked and swung open the doors, and the cool damp air was a relief that grew with each step down into the darkness. When my foot reached the musty collection of rugs and welcome mats that made up the wall-to-wall carpeting, I took a deep familiar breath and then tossed my ratty bag onto the rattier old couch.

You were right behind me and on one knee in an instant. Your eager, slender hands couldn't move fast enough, it seemed, to get that gig bag open and your Jazzmaster out and plugged in. I watched you work, laughing to myself quietly but so you'd notice.

You got to your feet and slipped the guitar strap over your neck and shoulders in one smooth move. "What?"

"It's like you've moved in," I said. "Yesterday you were like a frightened hamster coming down those steps. I had to hold your hand."

You waved me off. "All right, all right. Just get back there." You nodded toward the drum kit, so I obliged and grabbed a couple of sticks off the floor.

The kick was a little too far up, so I pulled it back and tried to get those pointy legs on either side to catch a little. I reminded myself again to find a cinderblock at the warehouse and drag it up here. For a minute I imagined my fingers, pulling them off the char-stained brick, covered in soot. Deep breath.

"What are we playing?" I asked, and you shrugged. Your back was to me as you adjusted your volume and slowly strummed through a few chords. "What's that you're playing?"

"Nothing really," you replied between strums.

"Well, let's make it something, then," I said, and I joined you. It was slow, then a little faster, and eventually we found a good tempo for the changes. When you slipped in a new change, I switched to the ride and let it be the chorus—the "refrain," Felix would have called it. A few measures later you went back to the original changes, so I dropped down a little and closed up the hi-hat. Then you started to sing.

There were no words—at least, I don't think there were—except now and then when you'd drop in something with sense. But it didn't matter. Your melody is what counted, and it counted a lot. It floated over the changes, above them. It wove through my rhythm and the chords you played, like a pixie through a crowd—better than them, more than them. In every way, the melody elevated the song until it almost felt complete, like it always would be complete: you just had to open your mouth and let it come out.

I opened the hi-hat just a little, to let it sizzle a bit, and leaned forward on the throne, closer to you and your voice. That voice—rich and sweet, crystal clear. Even over my drums and your guitar, I could hear every note, every trembling vibrato, every quiver, and it was glorious. Anyone would know you'd never smoked, and probably never would, because the moment you put a cigarette to your lips and a flame to its tip, a host of heavenly angels would snatch it away and throw it into hell.

The chorus came around again, so I moved to the ride, but you fumbled a chord change and your voice fell away. The angels retreated to their clouds and I shook my head as I snatched the cymbal to quiet it.

No more—no more love, no more songwriters, no more long and gorgeous fingers in my hair. Purity of voice and purity of heart doesn't mean purity of soul, and certainly not purity of body. You'd be gone in weeks, I knew, and I wasn't going to let you into my heart before then.

THE END OF IT

It was fun—playing music with you, playing house with you, there in Fish's cellar. It was always us or nothing: Almost no sound came in from the street, that end of Franklin as quiet as it is, without Fish's place to fill it up with sound, of revelry and of jukebox music. Sometimes a car boomed by, blasting Euro pop or Dominican dance. When one did, the little scene we had would break, but just for a minute, never long enough to make me, or to let me, think about it.

It was our third day in the cellar. I'd been out for a bit, picking up sandwiches with your cash, and when I got back, you were sitting on an amp, leaning on the brick column in the middle of the cellar and facing the ajar back door, strumming your guitar. I dropped onto the couch and pulled open the bag of food. "Is that another new song?"

You jumped a little at my voice; I guess I broke your little reverie. But you gave me a quick smile.

"Honestly, you're like a machine," I said, sitting down. I pulled out your cheese hero and leaned it over to you.

"Thanks," you said. You used the side of your palm to turn the volume of your guitar all the way down, then laid it on the rug beside you and slid down to the floor beside it to eat.

I shrugged as I unwrapped my Italian hero and took a bite. "Don't thank me," I said, letting a little food escape as I spoke. "You bought."

You smiled at me and shook your head, then patted a little mayo from under your bottom lip.

"So?" I said, avoiding your eyes with mine. "What was that you were playing?"

"Just a new song," you said, adding quickly before I could ask, "Not ready to share yet."

"Come on," I said. "We're a band, aren't we?"

"Or a duo," you said, and your wrist jangled as you lifted your butt from the rugs and leaned forward to fish your soda from the bag at my feet.

"That's a kind of band, not a non-band," I said. "So you have to share it with me."

"It isn't finished yet," you said.

"Then I'll help you finish it," I said, putting the second half of my hero down on its waxed paper on the floor and stepping behind the kit. "Come on. Just give me the changes and the rhythm. We'll bang it out."

"All right," you said in your grumpiest tone. But you got to your feet and pulled on your guitar and rolled up the volume. Your tone was extra sweet that day; tube amps are funny that way. "It's called 'Like Me.'"

I warmed up with a little snare fill, then a chunky thing with no backbeat. You were patient and I finally stopped, then looked at you and, with a smile, nodded.

Your eyes were on your hands and strings at first, as you pushed slowly through the pattern of changes and strums and open chords. The mic was off, so I couldn't make out your words—just snippets of melody and the movement of your lips in time with the music. Your voice wasn't carrying that day; you almost seemed shy. Sometimes your eyes came up and met mine, when your lips didn't move. But whenever you sang, it was all hands and strings, hands and strings, and I started thinking about marionettes—hands and strings.

I left the kick out of it for a while. Just some gentle ticks on the hi-hat and my brush on the snare, so my drumming sounded like rain and a watch at my ear, and I thought about the time we'd had and how much more we might get. I watched the stick in my right hand move up and down on the gold of the high hat. You stopped playing and I looked up at you.

"What?"

"You don't like it," you said.

"Of course I like it," I said. "I love everything you play. Everything you write."

You sat on the edge of the couch and turned the volume down to a squeak, then strummed through the changes again, quickly. "You didn't seem into it."

"I was," I said. "I just didn't think it needed much support from me, at least not at first. It could always build up, you know—toward the end."

You found my soda in front of the couch and stole a swig from it.

"Hey," I said with a smirk, kidding. But when you looked up I said, "Is the title a description, or, like, an order?"

You put down my soda and got back to your feet. "It doesn't matter which," you said. "Can we do it again?"

I nodded and clicked you in.

. . .

That was the end of it. The end of three days of pizza and deli sandwiches, and of my wondering how much money you had, and when it might run out. Three days of pulling the cellar doors closed behind us and creeping out to the garden, to lie on our backs and stare at the empty sky. Three days of music and sleeping deeply, with your hands on me sometimes. On the third night—late, probably, maybe after midnight—I woke suddenly. Your face was near mine in the dark, and I couldn't imagine how you slept so easy, so deep, in this weird place, away from everything you knew.

The ceiling creaked. Someone was up in Fish's— probably Fish, in her big black boots, stomping around after days away. That must have woken me, I realized, and I glanced at your face in the dark. You were still asleep, so I got up and found my jeans and, as quietly as I could, swung open the cellar doors to the sidewalk. In a crouch, I got to the window of the bar and peered in: there was Fish, pushing stools around, sweeping up, even collecting some empties that she'd left out in the hurry of the other night. She looked tired. I opened the front door and went in.

Fish was on her knees, reaching under the pinball machine for a couple of cocktail napkins, balled up, and a red swizzle stick. She looked up when the door closed.

"Out." She went back to cleaning. I watched her until she stood up and walked to the tall trash can at the end of the bar.

"Fish, I'm sorry."

"Out!" she snapped, turning to face me. I flinched. "Dammit, Kid. What are you even doing here?"

"I—"

"You've been sleeping downstairs again, haven't you?"

The floor along the bar was still unswept. I grabbed the broom leaning on the window next to me and started in.

"Don't."

But I did. I pushed at the dust and napkins along the bar and soon had a nice little pile going. I even found a few cigarette butts. I clucked my tongue. "Are people still smoking in here? That's illegal, you know." I let a little smile show in my voice.

"Stop, sweetie, okay?"

I shook my head. "This was the deal, remember? I help you clean up and you let me practice and sleep downstairs, right? Since the fire."

Fish watched me another minute. "No more sleeping," she said. "No more hanging around the bar when the drinkers are here. You need to be at home right now, Kid."

I shrugged as I pushed the broom around. "Maybe I do."

"I mean it," Fish went on. "When the serious drinking crowd is around—that includes Jonny—you and your new friend . . . and Konny . . . aren't allowed anywhere near this place. Just keep off the block. No practicing, and definitely no drinking. Do you get me?"

I stopped sweeping and leaned on the broom. "If I need to sleep here—"

"You don't."

"If I *need* to."

Fish sighed and went behind the bar. She pulled out two glasses and filled them with ice, then Coke. I grabbed one and took a long pull at it.

"If you need to," she said finally. "I mean *need*. I know your home life isn't ideal, sweetie. But do you know the fine I just paid?"

I shook my head and Fish grunted.

"Scout's downstairs."

Her fist came down on the bar. "No."

"I know," I said. I drank the last of that Coke and wiped the glass's sweat on my jeans. "We'll clear out. But we can still practice, right? When it's not a crazy alcoholic drugfest up here, right?"

"Ha ha," Fish said. "Just get."

I headed for the back door and pushed it open.

"Kid."

I turned around in the open doorway. "Yeah?"

"Did you start that fire?"

I looked at her and she pushed a chunk of hair out of her eyes and over her ear. It fell right back out.

"No."

PICK A DIRECTION

Fish's plan went well for quite a while. You and me were really a band, just the two of us, and even though we couldn't play house anymore, we could practice plenty, and that's all we both said we wanted. Of course, part of me—a lot of me—wanted more, but I kept that part quiet, drowning it out with an occasional thundering drum fill or stifling it with a lungful of smoke. After dark, we went our separate ways, and though every time we said good-bye I died a little, like Cole Porter, it also got easier and easier. Fish's plan was helping me keep my heart at bay, and keeping my body out of foster care. I was careful never to bump into my parents, but it was always obvious I'd been there. I'd leave a dirty dish in the sink, or leave a note for my mother. My dad might not have cared, but I had a feeling Mom would let the cops know I was still at home, if it ever came to the question. She didn't want me snatched up by the system.

But Fish's plan was too fragile. That was obvious two weeks into it. It was a little after midnight when the red lights flashed down from the street into the cellar. At first I didn't notice them; I'd probably drifted off, on a wave of your voice and guitar, and with Felix's Christmas lights pulsing along, who would have noticed some flashing lights anyway? Then came the heavy footsteps and sudden silence upstairs, punched now and then by two loud male voices.

"What's that?" I said, sitting up.

You had stopped playing—I don't know when—and your hand was on my ankle. You were humming softly when Jonny leaped in through the garden door like Errol Flynn.

"Kid!" He looked at you for a beat—lustfully, I'd guess, like a new toy—then back at me. "You two have to get out of here. Now."

"What's going on?" I asked. You got to your feet and laid your guitar across its amp.

"Fish is being raided. The number of fake IDs up there is astounding," Jonny said, shaking his head, still smiling. "But you, Kid—you gotta make yourself scarce. With everything going on, if they find you here it'll be a trip to juvie hall for sure."

I took your hand and started for the front steps, but Jonny held you back. "Not that way. There are two police cars that way. You're going over the fence."

I looked at him; my eyes must have been a mile wide.

"Come on," he said, and headed back out to the garden.

We followed. Jonny moved quickly, weaving through the crowd, the flashlight beams, the empty bottles of Rolling Rock and High Life. At the fence, he hissed at me and put out his hands, clasped, like a step, and I was up.

"Where are we supposed to go?" I asked, one leg over the fence, into a stranger's backyard.

Jonny gave you a boost. "I'm Jonny," he said quickly.

"Scout."

"Nice to know you," he said, his smile slimming a little under the stress. "I don't know, Kid. But Fish is pissed. She told you not to be down here this late. She's saying no more cellar, period."

"But—" I said, desperate.

"I'll talk to her. Just go!"

I hopped down and looked for where to go next. There was no route to the street; just more backyards and more fences, rows in every direction.

And then you and I were sitting in the darkness of a backyard, up against the fence. I felt your hand take mine, and the rhythm pulsed from my hand to yours, and back again, and my breathing slowed just enough.

"I guess . . . we pick a direction?" you said. You looked at me sideways and managed a smile, covered your mouth to suppress a laugh maybe.

I smiled back and nodded. Suddenly the floodlights in the garden behind us—Fish's garden—flared on.

"Right now!" I said, laughing, and we got up and ran for the fence to the right—it looked a little shorter.

. . .

We walked around Greenpoint for a bit and ended up heading east and south into Williamsburg.

"Want to watch a movie?" you asked as we made our way down Bedford. It was filthy with hipsters, as always: trucker hats, fur collars, ridiculous tea dresses, oversize sunglasses—never sincere, and I wondered what they were so afraid of.

"I'm not so into movies," I said. "Besides, where?"

"At the video store, down near North Fifth."

I squinted at you. "How do you know about that store?"

You smiled at me and gave me a little shove and giggle. "I haven't been in your little clutches every minute, you know."

"Just about!"

"But still not. And I like movies, so I found it. Here."

We went in. It was dark, darker than the street after midnight. The only light seemed to come from the TV set hanging low over the glass counter at the back. A gorgeous girl was sitting on a high stool, considering the TV and nibbling a strawberry shoelace. I grabbed your hand.

"I can't see a thing."

You led me toward the counter and said, "Hi, Lill."

She smiled at you, it seemed sincerely, and turned back to the screen. A dark-haired boy—sick-looking—

was hacking at another boy's hair with a dull switch blade. I knew at once it was *The Outsiders*. It's a terrible movie, really, but I remember watching it in ninth-grade English and marveling at how in love the two lead actors seemed: awkwardly and happily, but neither seemed to know it completely. I watched your face as the light from the TV flicked over it, and your lips parted just a little.

· · ·

"I better get home," I said, standing on Bedford. My hands couldn't get any deeper in my pockets if I tried, and I did try: some dizzying blend of keeping my hands to myself and pushing my jeans down.

"Oh, sure. Okay." Gig bag hitch.

"It's late, and you know," I said. "I gotta sleep there most nights. I'd rather check in at home than with social services if the police come after me again."

"Yeah, of course."

"What about you? Where have you been staying?"

You laughed and, even though your hands never left your pocket and the strap of your gig bag, you waved me off—the picture of casual. "Don't worry about it."

But I did worry. I left you there, on the corner of Bedford and North Seventh, and didn't look back until I passed the guerrilla garden—people taking back the nature they gave away in the first place—in a vacant lot across from a vintage clothing store. But I knew I wouldn't spot you through the Bedford Avenue masses.

ANYONE YOU WANT TO CALL?

I'd lost track of days by then, but from the noises in the apartment in the morning, I could tell it was a workday for both my parents. The clock radio on the floor next to my bed said 6:15, so I knew I had an hour or so before both my parents would be ready and gone. I leaned across to the window and pulled up the blinds to let in the sunrise, then I dug around under my bed for my sketchbook and some vine charcoals.

I sat for a minute with the pad on my lap, the end of a charcoal against my lips, looking around the room for something to sketch. Not much—I chose the lamp, standing on the cluttered desk in the corner, up against the wall, leaning over the pile of books and papers like it might learn something.

The charcoal moved across the newsprint quickly at first, long arcs that swooshed across the paper and sent a little shiver up my hand and my arm to my neck. I shook once and smiled, then kept going. The lamp took shape quickly, looking eager and a little tired. The clutter was a treat to draw, all shadows and shapes in dizzying perspectives. I was hovering over the pad, leaning close to the newsprint, where I could smell the paper—a little musty but clean, like a glass of water that sat on the nightstand overnight—when the apartment door slammed shut, with its familiar metallic sound and dainty click of the automatic lock, then the deep thud of the deadbolt.

I sat up straight and looked down at my pad, and then I realized: I'd been sketching you, really. I mean, I'd drawn the lamp, and the chaos on the desk, but I'd given it your soul. I'd given that lamp your optimism, your bright face looking down on all that havoc. I pulled the sketch off the pad and rolled it up, stashed it in the back corner of my closet for safekeeping. Then I wished I had been sketching on paper a little heavier than newsprint, hoped it would somehow survive, but guessed that it wouldn't.

. . .

Who knows the last time I'd been alone in that apartment. I kicked around for a while, checked out the fridge, made an egg sandwich for myself. I didn't get out of there until almost noon, right after I finished a can of beer and had flipped through all the TV channels enough times to remember how stupid they are. When I got outside, the sun was high and deadly hot. I shielded my eyes and wanted another beer.

"Kid!" It was Konny. She was across the street, sitting on the stoop, alone—waiting for me. And she was pissed off.

Konny got up when I stopped in front of my building. The B-48 roared down the street between us, then she stomped across. The earth probably trembled beneath her.

"Hi."

"First of all, Kid, what the fuck?" was Konny's opener. "I haven't hardly seen you since this new kid showed up."

"Scout?"

"Yeah, Scout," she said, snarling, spitting out the name. "Are we doing a little repeat of last summer?"

"Shut up, Konny."

"Okay, I'll shut up, right," Konny said, thick with snark, and my chest burned a little at the thought of her using it against me. "In that case maybe you can tell me why the fuck the police have been to my parents' place, asking about the fire at the warehouse."

"Huh?"

"Huh is right," Konny said, stepping a little closer to me, all six feet in high-heeled stomping boots of her. "There's a goddamn APB on my ass right now, did you know that? You did, didn't you?"

"No!"

"Do you think I'll be able to keep my job and my goddamn apartment if the cops start showing up at the comic shop, asking about me? What the hell did you tell them, Kid?"

"What do you think I told them?" I said. "They wanted to know all about the night of the fire, so I told them. . . . I told them I was with you."

Konny's jaw went firm and she looked at me hard. "I have to get to the store to open up."

Then she turned and stomped off.

I watched her walk away for a minute, then jogged after her. "Wait."

"I can't wait. I just said, I have to open the store."

"Then I'm coming with you," I said, struggling to keep up.

"Fine, come. Guilt is a wonderful thing for our friendship, huh?" she said, smirking, softening a little at the edges, I hoped.

The comic shop isn't far across Meeker from my parents' place. We rounded the corner onto Metropolitan, though, and stopped short.

"Shit," Konny said after she turned the corner onto Metro. "They're here now."

She was right. An unmarked police car was idling in front of the comic shop. "It's no big deal," I said. "They just have to talk to you. They'll probably track down Ace too."

"Ace?"

I shrugged. "I just popped off every name I could think of," I said. "Everyone I knew who maybe had seen me that night."

Konny looked down at me. I swear, her body cast a shadow across my face. "I thought you weren't even trying to dodge this rap. I thought you weren't denying anything. Why the alibi?"

"I never denied it. They asked me where I was that night, and I told them. They asked who I saw, and I told them that." Konny's eyes narrowed at me a little. She was furious, but I could tell it was at least a little phony, just for show. "That included Ace, at the park. Remember?"

She took her eyes off me and peered back at the shop. "Yeah, I remember that. The little shit."

"Let's just go," I said, taking her wrist. She let me lead her a few paces, then we walked side by side the rest of the half block to the shop.

"Well, isn't this a picture," one of the cops said as we walked up. His head was clean shaven, and I knew he was one of the cops who brought me in that first day of summer. Plus he seemed to recognize me. He smiled and said, "Two birds, one stone."

The other one dragged his eyes from Konny's astonishing physique to look me up and down. "Well, one bird, anyway. What the hell is that?" He nodded at me.

The bald one quieted him with a hand on his shoulder. "That's Kid, our fire starter," he said, watching me, and his smile fell. "We were planning on visiting your parents after seeing Konstantyna—I presume?—here, but this ought to save us the trip."

"Konny. Can I open the store?" Konny said. She threw her hip, it looked like to the second cop's delight, and held up her key ring.

The bald one nodded once. "You better," he said. "We'll talk in there. Kid, get in the car with Officer Stivic till we're through. And Stivic, be nice."

I watched Konny as she unlocked the gate then reached down to grab the bottom and toss it up. Stivic was ogling like crazy. I'd have worried about getting into the car with him alone, but I had a feeling I wasn't his type. He opened the back door for me, and I slid in and leaned on the far door.

"So, Kid," he said, heavily accentuating my name. "Haven't been home much?"

I caught his eye in the rearview mirror but didn't reply. He let out a chortle, then shrugged. "You've lived on the street. You look tough enough. I'm sure you'll be fine anyway."

I clenched my jaw and tried not to respond, but I couldn't hold it. "What are you talking about?"

"You gotta know social services is coming in on this thing," he said. "You ain't slept at home since we found you at that little bar on Franklin, am I right?"

"I slept at home last night!" I spat back at him. "I always sleep at home . . . practically."

He grinned at me, real big, in the rearview. "Am I supposed to believe your dad, or am I supposed to believe you?"

"You want me to answer that?"

He laughed at that for real, like it was the funniest thing ever. "Sure, Kid."

"Then me, believe me. I slept there last night. Come on, I don't want to go into foster care or a home or something. What good would that do?"

He turned in his seat to get a look at me. "You're sixteen years old, and you're looking at prison time, I'd guess, once we get this whole thing figured out. And you're sitting here worrying about foster care? Social services? Kid, you'll be lucky if you end up in a group home at this point, understand me? That is, unless there's something you want to tell me about the fire."

I didn't know what to say, so I let myself slump back in the seat and sulked until the bald cop climbed into the passenger seat a few minutes later. Konny stood in the open doorway of the comic shop, leaning on the jamb, and watched as we drove away.

I figured we'd head to my place, so the cops could talk to my folks. "My parents won't be home yet," I said. "Dad will be at the plant until six at least, probably till eleven for the time and a half."

"That right?" said the cop driving, the one with hair, the one with eyes—for sixteen-year-old Polish girls.

"Mmhm. And Mom's shift always goes long at the hospital. And they're both impossible to get on the phone. I doubt either of them will be around before eight at the earliest."

We were stopped at a red light, crossing over into Greenpoint from Williamsburg. When it turned green, we moved under the BQE onto McGuinness, but at Meserole we turned left, toward the river and the precinct.

"You're taking me to the police station?"

They didn't answer. Didn't even flinch. But we pulled up to the station into one of those funny diagonal spaces that make that street such a pain in the ass for everyone else. Then the bald cop pulled my door open and grabbed my elbow. "Let's go."

His humor was gone. I barely had time to lift each foot as he pulled me up the stone front steps and into the station. Once inside, my chin barely reached the booking desk. I'm sure there's some psychological reason to have the desk so freaking high. The officer at the desk held my fingers tight enough to hurt, and though I wouldn't have squirmed, I found I wanted to and did try to pull away, which only made him grip harder. I guess that's what they call a self-fulfilling prophecy.

"So this is the kid who burned the old warehouse down?" he said as he gave my left ring finger an extra tug. "My father worked in that warehouse, did you know that?"

"No," I said. I knew he probably wasn't really asking me.

The cop just gave me a long flat look. He was an ugly man, really: bad skin, thin hair of several tones of black and gray, streaked back with its own grease. His nose was bulbous and poxy, like he had some Dark Ages infection or a plague of boils or something. He went on to ask me lots of questions: "real" full name, address, sex. It began to dawn on me I might not be leaving the station this time, unless it was to be transferred to a real jail or something.

"Anyone you want to call?" He got up from his stool and came around the desk to take my arm and lead me through a swinging door toward the back. He deposited me on my feet against a white screen. Soon he was saying, "Look right," "Look left," "Straight ahead."

I stared at him across the top of the camera. It wasn't a boxy thing on a stand, like you see in movies. It was on a desk, and it was very modern-looking. I could see at an awkward angle the monitor, and each snap he took showed up right there on the screen, in full color. He barely glanced at me.

"My parents are at work," I said. "Neither of them can really take phone calls."

He didn't look up from the computer. He just asked me again: "Anyone you want to call?"

I could call Fish's bar, but I guess I knew how that would look to the cops. I didn't know how to reach Jonny, or anyone else, except Konny at the comic shop. I went with that.

"They arrested me."

"Shit." She inhaled and sighed loudly.

"What did they ask you?"

"You know, just where I was that night and stuff. I couldn't remember much. I remembered walking with you and seeing Ace, and then you running off. And I told them I sat with you on the curb while the warehouse was burning, and about Fish walking us away from there."

I nodded, then realized she couldn't see me. "I don't think I've talked to you on the phone since we were maybe ten, Konny."

She laughed a little, then said, "So what are you going to do?"

I lowered my head and my voice. "Would you run down to Fish's? Or call over there?"

"Don't you want your parents?" she asked. "I could—I don't know. I could go down to the plant. It's right around the corner."

I imagined Konny walking into the fish-packing plant, through the stench like a wall—and through about fifty Polish men, ages eighteen to eighty, I bet.

"Like he'd come to my rescue," I said. "Please? Just let Jonny know if he's around, or Fish if she can find him, I guess. Okay?"

Konny was quiet for a minute.

"Okay?" I said again.

"And Scout?"

I pictured your eyes and then your mouth. And your cheek as you chewed on that egg sandwich, jutting just a little, your lips pursed tight together. The plum after the first bite you took from it, its flesh redder than blood, juice on your fingers.

My head went even lower, and my voice, as my shoulders went up, pressing the old black handset hard against my ear. "Okay." It was barely a whisper.

Konny didn't reply, so I said another thank you and a good-bye and hung up.

The ugly cop wasn't watching me or listening. He couldn't have cared less. I shifted in the big wooden chair he'd put me in, next to an officer's desk and an open window, made escape-proof only with a heavy metal lattice. "I'm done."

"That's great," he said without looking up. Then I just sat some more.

. . .

Detective Blank turned up within the hour. I don't think anyone called him in on my account. He just happened by. When the desk cop caught him up, and after he'd spoken to the shaved-head one, he sat down at the desk by the window with me.

"Is this your desk?" I asked him.

"Sure," he said. "So what's going on today?"

I shrugged. "Well, I got arrested. How are you doing?"

He smiled a little. "You have a lawyer? Does your mom or dad have a lawyer or a friend who's a lawyer?"

I shook my head.

"An attorney will be provided for you by the City of New York, all right?"

I nodded.

"Social services is going to talk to you," he said. "A woman named Ms. Weinberg is in the interrogation room waiting for you. She's a good lady; she's worked with this precinct probably a thousand times. You'll like her."

"Okay," I said.

"You want anything?" he asked. "Water?"

"How about a Coke?"

He smiled at me. "There's a machine in the basement. I'll get someone to run down there and grab one for you, okay?"

"Thanks."

He nodded and started away. When I didn't follow, he turned around. "You should come with me now."

"Oh," I said, getting up. "Sorry."

He led me to a room down the hall—the interrogation room, but not the same one I'd been in with my parents. Inside was a small woman with long dark curly hair—beyond curly: kinky. She was looking through a folder—my file, I assumed—and sipping from a can of Tab.

The detective led me to a chair and I sat, then he stepped out. Ms. Weinberg said my name.

"Please call me Kid."

"Okay, Kid it is," she said. "I'm Ms. Weinberg. I'm a county social worker. It's nice to meet you."

She took another sip from her Tab and leaned back in her chair, legs crossed. "So?"

My eyes darted in my head. I wondered where my Coke was, if it was coming at all. "So what?"

She smirked and tried to toss her hair. It didn't budge. "Sew buttons. So did you start this warehouse fire? The whole city is dying to know."

"Come on."

"This was a big story," she insisted. "It's a mystery, and no one can move on razing the remains and building up the waterfront until it's solved. So did you?"

"Does it matter what I say?"

"What do you mean?"

"I mean, I'm here. You're here. The whole NYPD thinks I started the fire. Just ask the ugly guy at the booking desk. He just met me and he thinks I'm public enemy number one or something. He hates me. No one will believe me, and honestly I'm not sure I even care."

"You don't care?" she asked, already not believing me. I just shrugged, so she went on. "Maybe you're right," she said. She uncrossed and recrossed her legs. "Maybe no one will believe you. But the point is, from the point of view of the police, the case needs to be settled so the city can move on. Know what I mean?"

"That easily? Lucky for the city, huh?"

She laughed, and I let myself smile.

"Kid," she went on, leaning forward, "I'm here for you. Yes, I represent the county, but I got into social work because I want to be helpful to people like you. That's truth. Will you tell me some truth?"

"Okay."

"Did you start the fire?"

I took a deep breath and looked at the mirror behind Ms. Weinberg. "This is between you and me, right?"

"That's right," she said with a nod. "I'm not a police officer. Everything you say is confidential unless you tell me otherwise."

"Good," I said. "No."

"No what?"

"I didn't start the fire."

She looked at me, long and hard. "Are you sure? Remember, it's all confidential."

"You don't believe me," I said.

She put up her hands and smiled. "I do, I do. Take it easy. You didn't start the fire. Done and done. But that's not the only reason we're here."

"It isn't?"

She shook her head and took a sip from the Tab on the desk, using the opportunity to glance at the open folder next to it. "The police have picked you up at . . . a local bar? No name?"

I shook my head. "That's Fish's place, on Franklin."

"Fish?"

"She owns it. She's a great person. She cares about us."

Ms. Weinberg nodded, more at the folder than at me. "I'd like to meet her. Why do you hang around in a bar? You're only sixteen."

"It's a long story."

"I'm not in any hurry."

I laughed at that. "I don't know if I feel like telling it."

"That's okay too."

"Did anyone ever tell you you're very agreeable?"

"All the time."

I laughed again. "Fish lets me use the bar's cellar to play drums. That's the main reason, I guess."

"And because she's a great person."

"And that."

She considered me, maybe waiting for me to add something. It seemed like a cheap ploy, something they teach in social-worker school. I stayed mum. After some silence, she nodded. "Here's what happens now: we go in front of a judge. You'll have a lawyer. Did Detective Blank tell you about your right to an attorney?"

"Yes."

"Good. So, with your lawyer present, and your parents if you wish and they agree, we'll go in front of a judge—"

"When?"

She shifted a little, not uncomfortably, and said, "Hopefully tonight. They have court all night. Anyway, I'll recommend to the court that you be released into the custody of your parents. If you decide that's okay with you, you and your attorney will agree to those conditions, and I'm certain the city will agree to those conditions. Then the judge will agree, almost definitely, as well. Since you didn't start the fire, that will probably be the gist of it. I'll visit your home a few times, sometimes announced, sometimes not. I don't believe you are any kind of threat to society, nor to yourself. We'll work on how things are at home over the next few weeks, and months, and years, and next thing you know, you'll be eighteen."

"And that's it?"

"That's a lot."

"But I'm not going to jail?" I didn't feel relief, that's the weird thing. I felt guilty. Horribly guilty, like I'd gotten away with something I shouldn't have. But it wasn't the fire, I knew.

Ms. Weinberg shook her head, and her hair bounced just a little. "No way. Jail? Won't happen. We'll see what your parents have to say about your release to them. The worst case scenario right now? You're found guilty and your parents refuse custody. That would mean a group home, maybe foster care. But that's very unlikely and we can worry about that later if we have to."

I nodded, numb, barely listening. "Okay."

She got up and opened the door. "Detective Blank?" she called out.

He appeared a few seconds later holding a red can. "All through in here? The parents are waiting."

"I think we're through, yes," she answered.

Detective Blank handed me the Coke. It was super cold, and I snapped it open in a flash and took a swig.

He stepped back and leaned on the door, hands on hips. "I've been reading up on you, and on that bar on Franklin," he said. "I found something interesting about a connection you seem to have to a case from last summer.

Did we talk about Felix?" He shot a glance at Ms. Weinberg, then back at me.

I dropped my head and deeply examined my sneakers.

"Tell her about Felix," the detective urged.

Ms. Weinberg stepped between me and Blank. She glared at me. "Felix?"

"Tell her," the detective repeated.

I shook my head.

"Will someone tell me who Felix is?"

"Nobody," I said, hoping the matter would drop.

The detective didn't let it. "No," he said, laughing lightly, "not anymore he isn't. He *was* a local junkie, a street kid. Your boyfriend too, right, Kid? That's what I hear."

"From who?" I said, squinting at him.

"From who," he parroted through a chuckle. "From everyone who knows you. They all tell me how much that upset you, how rough this year has been on you. Not that I blame you."

Konny hadn't mentioned that on the phone, but I knew her: I knew how much she loved ranting about my love for Felix, my abandonment of her. She probably went on about him, on how much he mattered to me.

"Is that true?" Ms. Weinberg said, concern in her voice, mixed with a little strong anger. She was so feminine.

I shrugged. "It's been a shitty year, obviously. Look at me."

"Do your parents know about Felix?"

I shook my head.

She leaned back in her chair and sighed. "All right, let's get Mom and Dad in here."

Blank got up and swung the door open. They must have been right outside, because he mumbled briefly and they appeared. Mom looked about ready to lose it. She had both hands on my face in a flash, and blinked against tears.

"I'm okay, Mom," I said, and I pulled her hands from my cheeks. She sat at the table, and Dad sat next to me, but his expression was flat.

Ms. Weinberg gave a tight smile and said bluntly, "I'd like to release Kid to your care."

"Who the hell is Kid?"

I raised my hand at the elbow, shyly, and Dad chortled and shook his head.

Ms. Weinberg went on. "I'm going to recommend to the court that Kid get into grief counseling for at least a year. The county will supply a counselor, and the sessions can be held at home or at school. That would be up to you, to your family's schedule—"

"Wait," my mom stuck in. She sat up straight. "Grief counseling? I don't understand. There was a fire. No one died."

Ms. Weinberg eyed me gently, then said, "The three of you have a lot to talk about. I think Detective Blank will allow you to use this room for as long as you need it."

"Oh, sure," the detective stammered. "Of course."

Ms. Weinberg smiled at Blank and then at my parents. Then she patted my hand and smiled at me, sorrowfully.

I pulled away and dropped my hands into my lap. "Would the sessions be with you?" I asked.

She was leaning close to me now, and I could see something in her eyes, something I trusted. "No, I'm afraid. But I promise whoever it is will be completely qualified and very nice. Okay?"

I nodded once and let my eyes fall to my hands in my lap. Detective Blank opened the door and held it for Ms. Weinberg.

"And what if we don't want Kid?"

Everyone froze and looked at my dad. "After all, I never heard of anyone named Kid. Shouldn't be my problem, right?"

Mom crossed her arms. "Stop it," she said sharply.

Dad hardly looked at her.

Ms. Weinberg opened her mouth to speak, but the detective spoke quicker. "If you're refusing custody, I suggest you get yourself a lawyer. Our case for neglect is pretty strong right now, and if you refuse custody—with no significant behavioral issues to speak of—it'll be water tight."

Dad laughed. Mom got to her feet like she was ready to fight—or run out.

"No behavioral issues?" my dad said, still smiling, but somehow ranting too. "Do you call staying out to all hours, coming home drunk when at all, and burning down a goddamn warehouse 'no behavioral issues'?"

Mom moved toward me and I let her take my hand. Dad watched us a moment, then looked at me, not in the face. "And then there's this."

He paused, and I felt for an instant like a vase had dropped: a crystal vase was about to strike the linoleum floor of the interrogation room, and it would shatter and send shards into my eyes and Ms. Weinberg's face and my mother's gut. "I've got the only kid I know who doesn't know whether to be straight or gay or a girl or a boy or what." He turned to Detective Blank, but the detective couldn't make eye contact, or wouldn't. "You know the last time I let any of the guys down at the plant see my family? Five years, if a day."

The detective didn't reply. Ms. Weinberg stepped up to my dad and said, "You have the right to refuse custody. My advice is to retain an attorney. The county will not supply one for you, nor will the city, unless charges are filed against you and your wife for neglect. Until then, you'll want someone to represent you in court tonight. I still plan to recommend to the judge that Kid be released into your custody. Please discuss this with your wife." With that, she finally went through the door, which Blank had been holding open for this whole drama. He followed her and closed the door behind him, leaving my family alone to stew in our own juices.

Dad leaned back and crossed his arms. "Well, you know how I feel."

"No one was wondering," Mom said quietly. "You've made it very clear." I squeezed her hand a little tighter and she turned to me. "Talk to me."

I stared at her face for a moment, trying to remember my mother, trying to remember my home before life started to fall apart. It had been too long, but I had to start talking. So I did. And as I rambled on about Felix, and that whole summer and a year since, and the night of the fire, I began to recognize my mother again.

. . .

Court wasn't what I imagined. The room didn't look especially like a courtroom. There was hardly any wood, never mind ornate, dark wood. There was certainly no huge judge's bench, and no row upon row of benches, separated from the front by a gleaming banister. The judge was at a plain desk—it might have been pressed wood and aluminum. There were several chairs, enough for everyone to sit: me, Ms. Weinberg, my parents, Detective Blank, a couple of lawyers. The whole thing took only minutes. Ms. Weinberg gave her recommendation, my lawyer accepted on my behalf, and so did the county's. That was that. My dad might have turned a little red, but when it was over, we all went home together. Things were different now, though. I wouldn't have to leave again. I had Mom back.

ROT FOR SOMETHING

The next morning, once I woke up—late—I didn't dawdle. The night before had lit a fire under me, and though I wasn't sure yet where that energy was pushing me, I knew I had to move.

Dad had left for work by the time I hit the living room, and Mom was dressed and ready. "I'm a little late for work," she said when I came out of the bathroom, showered and dressed. "But I had to see you before I left."

"I guess Dad didn't have any similar sentiment," I said, but she waved me off.

"I'll deal with him," she said, like it was a minor hindrance. Mom gave me a stern stare. "Did you do this thing? Did you burn the warehouse?"

I looked at my feet, then quickly back in her eyes. "No."

She took a step toward me and nearly reached for my hand. "Why did you tell Dad that you did?"

I'd nearly forgotten. I had told him I'd done it, just to shut him up. I shrugged. "I don't know," I said. "To make him angry? Maybe I thought it's what he wanted to hear, or what he expected to hear, at least."

Then Mom did take my hand. She put her free hand on my cheek.

My eyes got wet, and I started to say something more. But I couldn't get it out.

"What?" Mom said.

"I think I wanted to be guilty," I said, and the tears started to really fall. "I wanted to rot for something."

She took me into a hug, our first in years. I let myself sink into it, and I wrapped myself under her arms and held her tightly.

"I never knew," she said quietly in my ear. "I never knew the pain you were in, the trouble in your heart. You're my baby, and you always will be."

"Why did you let me leave?" I said, not pulling away, as gently as I could. "Why did you let him make me?"

Mom pulled away suddenly, shock in her face. "Make you?" she said.

"Last summer," I said. "When all this started."

"I don't know what you're talking about."

I took a step back, widening the space between us even more. The backs of my legs hit the coffee table. "Dad packed my bag. I came home—late—and my bag was on my bed. Dad stood there and told me to leave. He said you didn't want me in your home."

Mom put her hand to her mouth and gaped at me. She hadn't known; for a year she'd thought I'd run away— run away to drink and get stoned and have sex. She'd been listening to Dad, and I hadn't been here to tell her some truth.

"Sweetie," she said, "I didn't know. I never knew."

Then she was crying, and I was, but inside I was light, totally weightless. While I thought she'd only taken me back in, she'd done so much more: she'd forgiven me, though I hadn't abandoned her; she'd defended me to my father, her husband; and now I knew she'd always be with me, no matter what.

. . .

The day was sunny and felt like the hottest of the summer so far. I wanted to run, or at least walk fast, but the heat had me loping along as though with Felix, like I was melting along the sidewalk, flowing down gutters to the river like wax. By the time I hit Fish's, it was after noon. The gate was up, and the front door stood wipe open.

Fish was behind the bar, leaning, and Jonny sat across from her, on the stool closest to the door. The jukebox played CD 22, track 5, and the room filled with Paul Westerberg's voice and piano. With that mellow little song and a near-empty bar, the place felt quiet and sacred.

"Hey," I said, embarrassed by the sound of my own voice.

There was the tiniest pause, after they looked up but before they registered it was me, and my chest was filled like a helium balloon. My mouth curved into a smile on its own, just as theirs seemed to, and then they were on their feet, at my side, arms around me.

I let them hug me, and I let Jonny plant kisses on my cheek. I let Fish take my wrist as she said, "Come with me," and led me through the bar and out the back door. She spun me around to face the closed cellar door. A sign hung there, made hastily from cut copper, and read Fish's Studio.

"What is this?" I said, staring at the sign, still smiling. My cheeks were beginning to go sore.

"A surprise," Fish replied. "I've been busy since those cops took you out of here. It took my lawyer and accountant and meetings at ungodly hours that end in 'a' and 'm,' but I got it done."

"I think you better explain," I said. "I've been through the ringer, and I'm feeling a little dense this morning."

"Afternoon," she corrected. "Here's the thing: the cellar is now a separate business from the bar. It's a rehearsal space. I can rent it out to whomever I please, for however much I please. And I'm renting it to you."

"For nothing?" I said.

Fish tossed her head a little and grabbed my hands. "You know, same old deal. You give me a little slave labor, and I throw you a little pizza, a little cash, and a place to play. But now it's all on the up and up. No more trouble with the whole bar thing upstairs. And it's licensed for all hours, as long as we soundproof."

"All hours?" I said, somehow smiling even bigger.

"To practice," Fish said, leaning down and closer to me. I wanted to kiss her. "Not to sleep."

"No worries there," I said, itching to get into the space and play. "I'm back at home for real. My mom and I are all square now."

"I'm glad to hear it," Fish said. She put her hand on my cheek and looked soft, just like my mom had at the station. I thought I'd cry for a second. "Then it's over? Is Kid's year-plus of hell over?"

"Not quite," I said, shaking my head lightly but holding her hand against my cheek with mine. "I still have to make sure everyone knows I didn't do it, that I didn't start that fire."

"Well, finally," a voice said from behind Fish. She turned around, and I looked past her shoulder, and there you were. A soft smile worked into your lips, and Fish stepped aside so you could run to me.

Your arms around my shoulders and your smell when I pressed my face into your nape were like a hundred-year sleep. I was completely at ease, completely refreshed. As we pulled apart just slightly, my face still against yours, Fish—she seemed miles away—said, "I'm going out to get soundproofing stuff. When I get back, you both help with installation. Okay?"

We nodded, smiling like idiots, and Fish went inside.

I found your cheek with mine and whispered in your ear. "I'm back at home. I think for good."

I felt you nod against me. "I'll go home too," you said, and I tensed. "I never planned to stay away, not for good."

I stepped back a little and held your gaze. "Where is home?"

"I'll show you someday," you replied. "Soon, I hope."

I nodded. "The end of summer's closing fast," I said. "It better be soon."

You laughed a little, but I just thought about last summer, and about Felix.

(SAYING GOOD-BYE TO FELIX)

There's a collection of five flat rocks just past the end of Quay. They sit like a couch before the reinforced and crumbling cement retaining wall begins. I'd sat there with Konny for years, since we were just little punks, kicking around and throwing stones and stealing tiny nips of booze from her dad's plastic jug in the freezer.

I'd sat with Felix there too, last summer. The warehouse was our home, and the five flat stones were our patio with a river view. The last time I sat at the river with Felix, with his head in my lap, it was nearly the end of that summer, the sky so gray and overcast that it felt lower, closer to our heads, and I fought the urge to duck. Still, I slouched under its weight.

Felix's eyes were closed, and his head rocked slowly back and forth on my crossed legs: no, no, no. He smiled slightly and hummed. I didn't know the melody, but could feel it was his own.

"Is that new?" I whispered. The river lapped up against the shore beside us. His head shake became a nod for an instant, then went back to no. His smile and hum never ceased. "I like it."

I pulled my eyes off him and over the river. I was facing north, toward the 59th Street Bridge—groovy—and the towers of midtown and the Bronx, our rival, like two beaten children fighting each other. Felix's melody was a slow waltz, and even though it came through his smile, there was nothing joyful about it, except in the way that remembering is joyful, that missing someone is joyful. Can you miss someone before they're gone, when they're still smiling up at you with closed eyes, and their beautiful face, with its deep-set eyes and two days of beard, is rolling slowly between your knees?

"I'm going to miss you." My voice was soft and cracked. I thought about the night we'd had, playing in Fish's cellar, my smiles as big as Jonny's, my shouts and shrieks nothing but joy, so frequent and careless that my throat was sore.

Felix's eyes twitched, and he reached up his left hand and put it against my cheek, so I held it there and finally smiled back at him.

FISH'S STUDIO

You and I played for a couple of hours straight, until we were both about to pass out from hunger. You leaned your guitar against the couch and clicked off the amp. "I have to eat," you said, reaching deep into your back pocket for your wallet. Your jeans hung low by the time you got it out and opened it up. You pulled out a few wrinkled, sorry-looking bills.

"This is the last of it," you said, holding up the loot.

"Let's make it good, then," I said, getting up from the throne. "And after today, I guess you'll have to get a job from Fish too, huh?"

You laughed a little. "Sandwiches?" you said. "Or Danny's?"

"Danny delivers," I said. "Let's make the food come to us. I'll call."

I went up to the bar, more crowded than it had been but still pretty thinly packed. The places with good sidewalk seating out front did a lot better until the night really cooled everyone off. It was still pretty early—not even dark yet. Fish still wasn't back, so I just grabbed the phone off the bar and hit the speed-dial for Danny's Pizza.

"Is this Fish or Kid?" came Danny's voice.

"Hi, Danny," I said. "It's me."

"What do you need? Plain large?"

"Yup, and bring it to Fish's Studio," I said. I hoped he could hear my smile.

"What the hell is that?" he said, Brooklyn to the bone. "You're at the bar. Caller ID, stupid."

I loved him to death. "Well the pizza's going to the studio," I explained, "under the bar."

"All right, all right," he said, "when you hook up the phone in the 'studio,' you let me know. Until then, I'm sending my delivery to the bar."

"Ah, you're no fun," I said. "Fine. Give it to Valentino." I glanced at the lion by the door, and he saluted to let me know he heard me.

"Now you're talking," Danny said. "Twenty minutes."

"Thanks."

. . .

After our late lunch, Scout and I leaned against the front of the couch and dozed. Between us, we'd polished off that whole pie, and with our bellies full and our musical appetites as sated—for now—we slept deep.

When Fish banged on the cellar doors, we woke up, you with your head in my lap, and I smiled down at you. "Fish is here."

You smiled back, then jumped to your feet as the doors swung up and open and Fish's big black boot appeared.

"Wake up, you little mongrels," she called down. "Give me a hand with this shit, huh?"

Fish brought all kinds of stuff: carpet fragments, egg crate foam, and even a few panels of what looked to be the real McCoy soundproofing material, like the kind they used in the music room at school. The work took us the rest of the afternoon. Fish had found a few staple guns, two hammers, and a bucket of nails, and we went to town, hanging everything everywhere: all over the walls, across the whole ceiling, even on the underside of the cellar doors and back door to the garden.

"This stays closed when the bar's open, okay?" Fish said sternly. We nodded and shot a few more nails into the panel of carpet that even covered the window to the back door.

"How am I going to breathe in here?" you said, and I quickly threw the back door open.

"Better?"

You nodded and smiled, and I glanced at Fish. She sighed. "Fine, if you need air, open the back door—just a crack."

You smiled at me and offered me your hand for a high five. I accepted and laughed.

"Nice to hear you laughing," you said quietly in my ear, so of course I stopped.

"But after tonight, no hanging out in the garden if the bar's open," Fish went on. "Outside that door is officially bar territory, got me? Kid, if you need to smoke, go out front."

"Bah, I'm quitting," I said, grabbing a big chunk of foam from the pile of materials in the middle of the room. "As of right now, I'm done."

"I'll believe it when I see it," Fish said. She started for the back door.

"Can Scout help out upstairs," I called after her, "with me?"

"Of course," Fish said over her shoulder. "Scout will owe rent too, am I right?"

You put a hand on my waist as I stepped onto a short ladder near the back door. I turned, and you held my eyes a moment. "I'm glad you quit smoking," you said. You looked at your feet and then tossed your bangs away from your forehead. "It was creepy—the lighting up, the lighters—little fires in your pocket."

"I guess," I said, and I found a couple of nails in my pocket to get started hammering the foam into the wall above the door.

"Anyway," you said as you turned away, "that's another thing settled, at least."

. . .

That day was our last in the back garden. Fish gave us a little reprieve, so after a quick jam to break in the new soundproofing, we joined Jonny out back for a couple of Cokes just as the sun was going down. When a group of smokers came out back, and Jonny headed inside, you and I retreated to the back fence. We leaned there, you and me, far from the small cluster of smokers; I couldn't stand being any closer or I'd light up myself, and for once I was serious about quitting. I was hot—sweating and breathless, and my face hurt from smiling. The Cokes tasted so good on the hot summer evening, and after playing drums for an hour, me and you just staring at each other over my crash, I drank the whole thing in one go.

"Your new songs are so good," I said, picking at a pocket of pebbles in the dry dirt next to my butt. "I hope we get a chance to play out this summer."

I snuck a glance at you beside me, hoping you'd pick up my meaning, between the lines: *If you're leaving at the end of the summer, we better hurry up and gig, huh?*

You might have, but I think your head was just someplace else. "Sun's almost down," was all you said, looking up over Fish's roof.

Another ending, I thought, wondering if that's what you meant, and I reached for a way to keep you here.

"I'll show you something," I said, leaning forward, overeager. "If you want."

You looked at me smiling and nodded, so I hopped up and brushed the dirt off my ass and then gave you my hand to pull you up. "Come on."

You followed me to the metal ladder that hung down from the fire escape. I grabbed one of Fish's cast-iron chairs and slid it across the patio, letting the scrape of the iron on the stone floor shriek and squeal for everyone to hear.

"Are you crazy?" you asked, smiling, and I smirked back and jumped onto the chair. On my toes, so my shirt came untucked and my belly showed, I could reach the bottom rung of the ladder up to the second floor. It came down with a clank and the smoking crowd turned to watch, some smiling with us, some baffled. You gave them a wink and put your finger over your mouth: *shhh*.

"Have you done this before?" you asked, grabbing the ladder and following me up to the second-floor fire escape.

"Once," I said.

(THE VIEW IS AMAZING)

Felix and me had played until after closing with no plans to stop and no idea of the time. I didn't even see Fish come in; suddenly her hands were on my sticks. I looked up and saw her angry face, eyes so narrow and tired that they were more red and black than their normal arresting and austere green.

"It's five in the goddamn morning," she said. Her voice was harsh and hoarse.

Felix's guitar rang out, hanging on a very big G7.

"I guess we lost track of time." I leaned over and switched off Felix's amp. It clicked and the volume dropped with a thud. Without the amplification, Felix was free to continue strumming, and he did.

Fish nodded at Felix, then turned back to me. I got up from the throne to put away my sticks. "Go *home*, okay, Kid?"

"Yeah, I will." I dropped onto the couch and pulled open my bag to find my cigarettes. "Promise." Lying liar.

Felix shook his head as he strummed and his lips stretched into his Cheshire smile. "Never promise." He sang it, like life was his personal opera.

Fish rolled her eyes. "I'm locking up the bar, both doors, and going home. Felix, lock this cellar when you leave, and the garden door. And, please: leave."

Felix stuck up his thumb at her and Fish shook her head and left. I lit my cigarette and went over to the back door to enjoy it, slipping my pack into my back pocket.

"I can't believe it's so late. We played for like five hours straight." I looked at Felix for a second and he was looking past me—maybe through me. I turned and blew a lungful into the garden. The darkness behind Fish's place—out over the rest of Greenpoint and beyond—was already fading. The slightest orange haze was forming, out over the water treatment facility past Provost Street.

"Want to really see it?" Felix had come up behind me. He put his small hand on my shoulder and I turned around. He slid past me and grabbed one of Fish's cast-iron chairs. There was a loud clank, and he was scaling the building.

"Felix!" I hissed up at him, but he didn't look back. He didn't even slow down. The rungs of the fire escape ladder were narrower than I thought they'd be, and my fist closed over them awkwardly. The paint was peeling and sharp. I let go immediately and wiped the flakes of blood-red paint onto my pants, then tried again.

Felix was already on the third-floor fire escape, and still going up, to the roof. I climbed to the second floor, as quietly as I could. When my foot hit the iron slats at the top of the ladder, I kept my eyes on the dark window. The curtain was open, and a broad-leafed plant was pressed up against the glass on the inside. A ragged, weather-beaten teddy bear leaned against the brickwork on my side. I started up the steep steps to the third floor.

Felix was already out of sight by the time I thought to look up for him again. Right overhead, the sky was still a deep indigo, and the brightest stars were still visible. The brightest stars were the only ones that were ever visible, and you'd have to stare for a long time before you see them—most nights the night sky was just a charcoal smear across the sky, no stars at all.

The last ladder was the longest, and it curved up over the edge of the roof. It was bolted into the bricks and reminded me of the wide-runged, slip-proof ladders out of the pool. Those only have two or three rungs, though, even in the deep end. This ladder had about ten—it felt like a hundred.

When I was able to peek over the top, Felix was right there. He put out his hand and smiled at me. "Turn around," he said when I was on the roof, on my feet.

I waited a moment to let my feet get the feel of the roof. It was softer than I thought it would be. It gave under my weight a little, like the ground under the jungle gym. Then I turned, and I could see the dome of the church on Manhattan Avenue, and the spire of the next church way up on Driggs. I could see the tanks and vats at the water treatment facility, and the BQE winding toward Sunnyside and Woodside and the Long Island Expressway, east.

And over it all was the blazing sunrise. Felix stood next to me and dropped his head onto my shoulder. I wrapped an arm around his waist. "It's amazing," I said. "Thanks for bringing me up here."

I felt him shrug against me. "I like the sunrise," he said. "But I prefer the sunset, because at least it's honest."

"What do you mean?"

"The sunrise is the rebirth, the promise the sun makes every morning: 'I'm here to stay,'" Felix said. "But it's bullshit. Because every night, it just leaves again."

I stared at the sunrise and my eyes got wet. I pulled away a little, just so I could use my arm to reach into my back pocket for a cigarette.

"The truth is," he said as I lit it, "the sun never sets and it never rises. It just keeps moving, all the time. It doesn't care about us."

I turned to him and blew my smoke out of the corner of my mouth, to the east.

IT ALWAYS COMES BACK

That night, you and I stood on the soft tar of the roof, a few steps back from the edge, looking out over Franklin Avenue and West Street and the husk of a warehouse. The Manhattan skyline was set in an aura of orange and gold and purple and red.

"There it goes," you said. It was already lower than the Empire State, the Chrysler Building, the Citicorp Building.

I dragged my eyes off the view and turned to face you, though you didn't notice. You didn't notice that my eyes had gone moist as I slipped my hand into yours and you squeezed it.

"New Jersey can have it," you said, smiling, your eyes still on the sunset. I dropped my head onto your shoulder. "It'll be back in the morning. It always comes back." And you turned and turned me with you, your arm around my shoulder, to look out over churches and highways and Long Island, at the deepening indigo where the sun would appear again in the morning, feigning devotion.

PEOPLE

The last few weeks of summer went by fast. Fish's cellar was all ours, but two things hung over my head. One was the fire, and the itch in the back of my head that some guys on the force still thought I'd done it. The other was you, and your impending disappearance. It was one practice, as the summer was dwindling, when we were sharing a pizza—compliments of Fish this time— that you said through a mouthful, "We need a name."

I leaned back against the front of the couch and let my toes in socks press against your knee. "What sums us up?"

You chewed that for a minute. "Freaks."

"Probably taken." I pushed myself up and onto the couch, then sprawled out across it. "How about the Runaways?"

"Joan Jett!"

"Oh yeah." I rolled onto my stomach and let an arm hang off the edge, picked at the carpet fragment disguised as a rug. "What are your songs about? I mean, in general."

You shrugged and dropped a folded crust into the box, then leaned back on your hands. They were probably greasy with pizza and for a second my heart skipped as I thought about licking the sauce from your fingers.

"Just the world in general, I think. You know, people."

"People it is."

"As a name?"

I smiled. "Why not?"

So we were People. Finally.

. . .

Our breaks usually had us wandering aimlessly, or else just lying around in the cellar, wishing for an air conditioner. That afternoon it was too hot even to wish, so we went out the sidewalk cellar doors and walked—more like a prance, really—away from the steamy cellar and into the cooler, drier air. Both of us buzzing on the music, we held hands and moved slowly west. I don't know how you felt, but I imagined it was just like me. I was so light and aware, like my skin and hair were electric and I could have moved with my eyes closed, with cotton in my ears, seeing and hearing better than I ever had before. My heart swelled with every step, and I decided to take you to the warehouse. I wasn't trying to be morbid. It was my old place—my home, really.

The high, temporary chain-link fence was still up and woven with yellow tape, but it wasn't any deterrent, not to us, not to the men who wanted a place to sleep or to drink without being bothered. But I wasn't thinking about them. I felt happy and high, weightless. The weeds among the ruins on West changed the smell of Greenpoint, just for a few blocks, and it hit me like last summer. I smiled.

"I want to show you something," I said, and gave your hand a squeeze before I let it go. Then I ran to the fence.

"Hey!" you called after me, smiling—I could hear the smile, and in my mind I could see your eyes, wide and aware.

I bent down and lifted up the fence at the bottom; it was lazily installed and easy to get past. I crawled under, then turned and held it up for you. You followed me, and I let it snap back down.

"The famous warehouse," I said. I put my hands on my hips and surveyed the warehouse, blackened and empty. I thought about that night and Konny and Fish, and about the couch in Felix's room. It would be gone now, maybe a few coils and nails in a heap of charcoal and shrunken synthetic cloth.

You came up behind me and I leaned back. "I heard about it back then. I hadn't realized it was right here," you said. "Not before I met you, I mean."

It had been all over the news, I knew. The thing burned and burned for two days. Still, I was surprised you'd known about it. I was surprised anyone had, outside of the neighborhood, like when a girl in art class had heard about Ace's cheating on Konny, or when the rest of the country slapped NYPD hats on their collective head five years ago, like it was their business.

I remembered that I still didn't know where you were from. I had guesses: Long Island? Jersey? The moon? I reached behind me and grabbed your hand to pull you along, toward the remains. "Come on."

"We're going in there?" you said. "Is it safe?"

"Not at all," I replied, laughing, and led you to the loading bay Felix and I had always used, and that I'd used most nights alone too, until May. It was brighter in that first chamber now, since so much of the roof had burned away. The windows had all been smashed out, probably by firefighters, and boarded over. Nearly all the boards were gone, though, by now. The one that had once blocked the loading bay was the first to go, just a week or so after the fire.

You climbed in behind me, with your shining eyes wide, and your mouth open in wonder. I recognized that look, because I must have had it all over my face when Felix first took me deep into the empty warehouse the previous summer. It was a different place now; when I put out my hand to stable myself, stepping over an I-beam, it came back black with soot.

I stopped between the two sets of stairs. Both still stood, but it was hard to tell if they led anywhere, or simply to a burned-out second floor. "I lived up that way," I said, pointing to the set on the right. "Those other ones led up to this crazy homeless man. He tried to kill me, pretty much." I rubbed my elbow a little, as if I still had the bruise the empty bottle had left.

You walked over to the bottom of the forbidden staircase and craned your neck to get a glimpse. "Do you think he's still up there?" you asked with mischief in your voice.

I shrugged, kicking around at the bottom of the other set, itching to go up, see what was still in my little room. "Jonny's throwing a party on Friday night."

You took a step up the forbidden stairs. "Yeah?"

I nodded, though you couldn't see me. "It's an end-of-summer thing. A last chance to see some people and have all the fun he can before people start disappearing, next week, I guess."

"That sounds like something we should go to," you said. "I'll miss some of those people too."

I turned to face you, sensing you'd finally stopped craning to see upstairs, and you were looking back at me. "Hey," you said. We looked at each other for a long moment. I couldn't speak, thinking about you leaving, heading back to the moon at the summer's end, like Jonny always did, or like Felix did, just once. When I took a step toward you, you suddenly smiled and said, "Catch me." And you took off upstairs, skipping every other step.

"Wait!" I called, running after you. "He might still be up there." I came to a stop at the bottom and listened to your laughter.

"I'm going to miss you," I added in a whisper, and the Polish man was nowhere to be found. Standing there at the bottom of the steps, I realized I knew some truth about the fire.

(MORE ABOUT THE FIRE)

It was early one night last summer, just as the sun was going down and the air off the river smelled a little nice and cooled my neck a bit, when Felix and I were strolling back to the warehouse. Fish's place had gotten crowded, so it must have been a Friday or Saturday, and the stomping over our heads was screwing up our practice.

"You could probably have gone upstairs," I said to Felix. "Done a set."

He shrugged off the notion and pulled out his cigarettes as we hit West Street.

"Spare one?" I asked, and he could and did. He lit mine with his, and I took a long slow drag and let it loose toward the river. We were close then, me and Felix. I probably loved him as best as I knew how.

"What the hell is this?" Felix said. I found what he'd seen: a little forest-green car parked near the bay where we usually entered the warehouse. When we reached it, Felix peered in the windows.

"Who knows," I said. "Some suburban kid looking for a party, probably got lost."

"And left his car here?" Felix said. I just twisted my mouth up a bit and hopped up onto the loading dock. I sat there, watching Felix check out the car. "Besides, this is no kid's car. It's too classic."

"I guess," I said, not really caring. I never got cars, or their appeal. For a second it seemed odd that Felix did, but with all his talk of leaving town, I guess it made sense. "Doesn't seem like it belongs here exactly, huh?"

Felix shook his head. "Not one bit, even."

I got comfortable in the dock, leaning against the wall and enjoying my cigarette. The heat wasn't so bad, fully in the shade now from the setting sun.

"There's a bunch of papers on the passenger seat," Felix said.

"What kind of papers?" I asked, but I wasn't really interested. It was just sort of fun watching Felix get into it.

"I can't tell," he said. "One of them says 'something something Construction.'"

"There ya go," I said. "Someone casing the warehouses to knock 'em down, put up condos. You know, like all over Williamsburg."

Felix must have been thinking that over. After a minute he said, "Yeah, probably."

"You all right?"

"Sure."

I took a last short drag and tossed my cigarette into the weeds. For a moment I thought it might start a little fire. It didn't. "You worrying about where you'll sleep if this place is gone?" I asked.

"Nah," he said. "There's always someplace to sleep."

I started to worry, though. I started to think about losing the warehouse, about the owner of this car showing up and catching us here—a couple of urchins. He'd probably beat us up, skinny and weak as we were. "Let's get inside."

Felix took one more long look into the car. "It's a nice car."

Then he jumped up into the bay and I got to my feet. Together we found our staircase and headed up to our room. We had company.

He wasn't tall, and he wasn't intimidating at all, outside of his obvious money: his clothes were expensive but ugly. His face was fat and smooth, and his hair was thin and slicked back, like he'd just gotten bigger and learned to walk—a giant baby.

"Who the hell are you?" Felix said, but it was obvious: he was the owner of the little green car parked outside.

The man didn't smile, didn't try to ply us with words. He just looked at me and Felix in turn. "Do you live here?" he asked.

"Yes," Felix said. "But you don't."

"I'm thinking about it, though," he said. "Thinking about buying this warehouse—the whole block, actually."

"So don't you have people who come check this sort of thing out for you?" I asked. "You're getting your shoes dirty."

He smiled at me slowly and went mum.

"Well, it's a shit hole," Felix said.

The man looked back at Felix for a moment, then moved over the little terrace at the back of the room. Stepped out onto the wrought iron and looked at the river. "A historic shit hole, in point of fact," he said. "Historic property equals headaches to people like me."

"So?" Felix said, and I thought about all those men in brown shirts, or navy blue, or maybe deep, forest green, grunting and sighing and laughing and shouting, pushing carts and hauling boxes, sorting and storing—taking smoke breaks out on the loading bay, just like me and Felix.

"So," the man said, turning around to face us again, "if I were to buy these warehouses, I'd have to bring them up to code, keep them intact, relatively speaking, in order to convert them, make them useful again."

"As condos?" I put in. "We don't want any more of those." I sat down on the couch and Felix tossed me his pack. I pulled one out and lit it. When I took a drag and sent my exhale toward the visitor, it meant: *You can go now.*

He laughed and took a cigar from his pocket. "I assume you don't mind?" he said, glancing at me with a smirk. Then he bit off the tip and spit it on the floor—

right on the floor—and lit the stinky thing. Smelled like shit right away.

Baby Face puffed at his reeking pacifier. He glanced around Felix's and my little place, looking at the little piles of trash here and there on the floor. He smiled briefly, then dropped his cigar right into a paper bag of Burger King wrappers. It burst into flames.

"Whoa!" he said through an open-mouth smile. He was laughing when I jumped up from the floor and stomped out the fire.

"What the hell?" I shouted, one foot slapping the concrete floor over and over, fragments of black, burnt paper floating around my ankle.

"Hey, don't blame me," he said to me, still smiling, his hands in front of him in defense. "This place is a fucking tinderbox."

I stood there, gaping at the psycho millionaire. He was done with me, though, his point having been made. He looked at Felix, and Felix's eyes glazed over as he stared back.

"If anything should happen here," he said, his face now serious and dark, "I'll know who to thank. I can be very grateful when I have call to be."

Felix put his cigarette in his teeth and wiped his palms on his pants, back and forth on his thighs several times.

"Are we clear?" the man asked, still with the hard stare at Felix.

Felix stood up and nodded slowly. "Absolutely," he said. "Do we shake?"

The rich guy smirked and pulled a new cigar from his coat, then put it in his teeth. "That's not necessary," he said. "Good night."

Then he turned and left our little room with a view. I sat there on the couch, watching Felix bounce nervously and listening to the real-estate investor's heavy steps on the way out. I hoped silently that our insane drunk friend would heave an empty in his direction.

"Are you serious, Felix?" I asked. He continued to bounce and fidget, and I could tell his next move would normally be to reach inside his pocket for a little rubber-banded baggy. "Felix."

My insistence snapped him from his trance of nerves and excitement and pre-needle. "What?" He stopped his kinetics and faced me.

"You can't be seriously talking about taking a payoff from that fat fuck to burn down the warehouse!"

Felix flashed an open-mouth smile at me. He even opened his eyes past half-mast for an instant. But his mind—his mind was as gone as it ever got, and that's saying a lot. He reached one hand out to me on the couch and squatted in front of me so I was looking down at his narrow, unshaven, beautiful face. And even though he stopped smiling, his eyes remained as big and bright as I've ever seen them.

"Kid, do you know what this could mean?" he said, putting his extended hand on my knee. A muscle twitched in my thigh. "One little flick of my lighter," he went on, snapping his thumb and first finger together, "and I could get out of here. I could go anywhere, do anything!"

I dropped my gaze from his eyes for a moment and he quickly spoke again. "You'd come too, Kid. You earned your freedom, right? You've still got plenty of it left too. We'll record, hire a full orchestra. You called me Brian Wilson, right? California, Kid. We could buy a place, studio time. This is what we've been wanting. Can you imagine?"

I shook my head and pushed his hand off my leg. I was mad at him, but also I thought if his hand crept another inch I'd let him do anything he wanted—and I don't just mean burning down the warehouse. When he sat back, I got up from the couch and headed to the terrace. "Listen to yourself, Felix." I backed out onto the terrace and leaned against the wrought iron. "I mean, I'm not going to get all emotional about the warehouse, but you can't seriously be considering doing this."

"Why the hell not?" He got up and lit another cigarette.

I rolled my eyes and turned to face the river. "Because it's stupid. You could get arrested. You could die! And honestly"—I spun to face him—"even if you get away with it and don't kill yourself or anyone else, he'd probably never pay you."

He waved me off and dropped onto the couch, then reached into his pocket for a fix. "Come on," he said. "Why wouldn't he?"

I stomped toward the couch. "Why *would* he? What are you going to do, sue him? Take him to court for breach of contract?"

"You're being melodramatic," he replied, not looking up from his habit. He was too busy digging around for his spoon.

"Fine," I said. "I'm going for a walk. Don't burn it down until I get back."

I had nothing to worry about, of course. I knew I'd come back in an hour to find him slumped over, passed out on the couch.

WHAT ABOUT YOU?

I almost kissed you that night. I thought it could be our last night. We were sitting on the windowsill in Jonny's apartment—at his end-of-summer party—looking out into the heart of Greenpoint. I watched you purse your lips when you sipped your drink, and I thought, *We could kiss.*

Past your face—it looked more beautiful to me by the minute—Greenpoint's sky was as dark as it gets, hued in green and pink and white, from streetlights and phosphorescence and the world past its close horizons. We hardly spoke, because all night "good-bye" tried to find my lips from where it was stuck in my throat, like a pill that wouldn't go all the way down, so I pushed it back with sip after sip of my drink.

Your hair fell over your eyes a little bit like it does when you sing and play guitar, when your hands are too busy in the moment to push those bangs back up. I looked down into my drink, which was mostly ice at that point, but instead of looking back up and into your eyes, I just swirled it around, sending the ice in circles around the bottom of the cup. My lips went dry, and then my mouth.

"I'm getting another drink," I said.

You looked at me and might have smiled. "Okay."

Jonny was at the drinks table, flirting with Ace. I thought Ace was with some new girl most of the time lately, and I thought about Konny. I knew they were broken up, but I wondered if me and Konny were still even friends.

"Hi, Jonny," I said.

He gave me a shout through that open-mouth smile he uses. It always makes me a little fluttery, I admit, like I have to throw my arms around him and just get lost in there.

"Hey, Kid," Jonny said. He was drunk, and he bowed deeply, his best Prince Charming. "What has torn you from your window and moments with Scout?"

I held up my cup. "Drinkies?" I was already buzzing too, but Jonny would oblige.

Ace looked over my shoulder, toward you and our window, and I resisted the urge to follow his gaze. Instead I watched Jonny pour some plastic-jug vodka into my plastic red cup. He added plastic cranberry juice and a plastic fluorescent pink stirrer. "Thanks, Jonny."

"One for Scout?" he said, holding up a new plastic cup and a smile.

I looked back at you by the window, still alone, still staring out. You pushed your hair back finally and looked over at me. Your eyes were sad and faraway—I guess they usually are—but you tried to smile.

"I think it's time for us to go," I said. "Sorry, Jonny."

"Take care of that one," he said, leaning in gravely. "We all worry about you two, you know that, Kid?"

"I know," I said, handing him my drink back. "Thanks, Jonny."

I reached you just as Ace did. He leered at me and he was obviously drunker than usual, because he never looks at me like that—like a hungry lion sizing up a wounded antelope. I grabbed your hand. "Wanna go, Scout?"

"Rude much, Kid?" Ace said.

"Fuck off, okay? We're leaving."

I prayed a little, I think, that you would come with me and not stay with Ace to finally give him what he'd probably wanted all summer. Which was stupid, because of course you came with me.

We walked away together, and though I looked back at Ace, you didn't. You were gone—off in Scout brain. Ace was lighting a cigarette and waving at us, and through his teeth he called after us: "I love you, Kid!" Very singsongy and sarcastic; I wanted to punch him.

I knew I should have headed home. I should have dropped you someplace safe, or even left you with Jonny, but I couldn't say good-bye. Instead I pointed us toward the river. We walked embracing, down Driggs and across

McGuinness, and that's when you started talking. You slipped your hand around my waist and into the loop of my jeans and talked on, nearly clear across Greenpoint, and when we got to the practice space under Fish's, you passed out on the floor and I curled up beside you.

In the night, I dreamed you rolled over and kissed me on the mouth. I dreamed that my hands found your body and that we tore into each other like Christmas presents. But when I woke up, I was fully dressed and you were gone.

"Kid."

Something jabbed me in the side and I jumped a little. "Ow. What the fuck." I sat up. It was a boot, a big black boot. Just above it was a muscular calf and thigh, covered in ink.

"Kid, wake up." It was Fish, obviously, and she was angry. With a very loud sigh, she shook her blue bangs out of her eyes. Then she kicked me again.

"Hey! Just stop kicking me."

"You left the cellar doors open again."

I looked at my feet and remembered my sneakers were under the couch. I reached under to grab them and also found your orange glittery pick and grabbed that too. While I was sitting on the floor lacing up, Fish sat down on the couch behind me. "Listen, sorry for the rude awakening, Kid. I'm glad you're safe, but if anything happened to you or Scout . . . I mean, besides the legal trouble we'd be in, you and me—"

"I know."

"Okay," she said.

I got to my feet and looked down at her. "So, you didn't see Scout, huh?"

Fish shook her head. "But I have good news," she said. "And just in time too; summer's almost over."

I swallowed and turned away, thinking about the end of last summer, and your arrival when the summer began, and wondering again what the end of summer must mean.

"If People still wants to play upstairs, you can have a set tonight. Right at midnight."

"No shit?" I said, spinning to face her again. She was beaming. "A Saturday night?"

Fish shrugged. "I had a cancellation, to be honest, but I miss hearing you through the floor since we put up that soundproofing. You two were sounding so good—Scout's singing is pretty amazing."

I smiled. "I know."

"So, find Scout. Make sure you're here by like eleven, okay? I don't want to put out the sixteen-plus sign if I don't have to, know what I mean?"

"No problem," I said. For all I knew, though, you'd skipped town already. Maybe you hated good-byes as much as I did, and figured ducking out before I woke up was the best thing. I headed for the steps and up to the sidewalk.

"And for chrissake, Kid," Fish called from behind me, "lock the damn doors behind you!"

The sun was already pretty high. Saturday, not yet noon, and that night would be our last Saturday before school would start up again. And we had a *gig*. Meanwhile I hardly knew where I'd be come sunrise on Monday—maybe on my way to homeroom. And when I'd asked you, "What about you?" . . .

. . .

Do you remember when I asked, "So, what about you?"? We were walking hand in hand up Driggs. We'd split the little whisky in your flask and figured we'd find Jonny and get another drink.

Do you remember the sun was over the Royal Oak, bright as yellow, and we weren't sure if it was coming up or going down?

Do you remember that my shoelace tore on my right sneaker and we stopped at that bodega on North 12th Street and they only had black dress laces? You rolled your startling eyes and said, "That will have to do." The old Polish man behind the counter had been sleeping and our humor was too high for him.

Do you remember Jonny always left a ten-foot pole just inside the gate of his building? We grabbed it together and balanced it nearly straight to the sky to tap his window. He threw it open and stuck his head out, bare-chested and laughing with his mouth wide open, happy to see us. He wasn't alone, because he never is. But he dropped a key anyway.

Do you remember? I asked, "What about you? Don't tell me your story if you don't want to, but tell me your future. Where will you go when the summer is over?"

You grabbed the key off the pavement and slid it into the doorknob. "It's ages away, Kid. It's the rest of our lives from now." You pushed open the door, and I followed.

Do you remember that I took the open door from you as you shot up the steps, probably thinking about Jonny and a drink and finding out who he had up there tonight? But I waited until I heard him greet you before I started up, because the rest of our lives didn't feel very long to me, and I was thinking of you, and Felix, and another nine long months waiting for my heart to shrink again.

TWENTY-FIVE CENTS

I wasn't sure where I was heading, but I thought down to Williamsburg was the place to go. I stopped at the corner at Greenpoint and Manhattan avenues, right next to the steps to the G train, and saw Ace walking toward me with his new girl. Before he could spot me, I ducked into the shallow entrance of the corner store, behind the newspaper racks and displays of fruit salads on ice, next to a pay phone, covered over in stickers and tags and escort ads. It struck me to check my fifth pocket for change, and I found some and dialed my parents' apartment—my apartment.

My father never answers the phone.

"It's me." I kept an eye on Ace and his girl as they crossed against the light, at a jog, scowling. Ace's girl fiddled with the magazines.

"You didn't come home last night, did you?" my mom asked. I admitted it. "I can't do this again. I really can't."

"I know. I'm sorry," I said. "I didn't mean to stay out. But, well, summer's almost over. Next week I'll be back in school, and . . ."

She let me breathe for a minute. It's one of the best things about a mom, I guess: even at my age she knows my soul better than anyone, so when I don't talk for a minute, for five minutes, she lets me breathe.

"I had to say good-bye to a lot of people," I finally said. "To one person."

Now Mom breathed, and I let her. My patience wasn't as good as hers, though, so I pressed her. "Mom?"

"I'm here."

"Is everything okay?" I turned my back on the street and Ace as he and his girl walked past and into the store.

"Yes," she said. "Who is this one person?"

"Just someone I met this summer," I said, then quickly added, "a guitar player."

Mom sighed deeply. "Are you in love?"

"Mom," I said, or whined.

"Okay, okay."

We let the word "love" sit there on the line for a while. Then the recorded voice of an operator let me know I was out of time.

"Mom, I'm out of time on this pay phone," I said. The operator began to count down from five seconds. "I have to hang up."

"Okay, sweetheart. Thank you for calling." Four.

"Of course," I said. Three. "I love you, Mom." Two.

"I love you." One.

Zero. Click.

Twenty-five cents doesn't buy much in Brooklyn. But that was a deal.

. . .

What little was left of the morning had slid by quickly. The stores and fast-food joints were open already, the pizza places even had a few slices missing from their lunch pies. I passed three before I finally caved at the fourth, just near the corner of Bedford—my favorite anyway, thanks to Danny. He was working and he asked about you. I told him I hadn't seen you, not since last night.

"We're playing down at Fish's bar tonight, though," I said. "Don't heat it up," I added quickly before he tossed a room temperature slice into the oven. He obliged. "Thanks. Anyway, Scout will be there tonight for the show. You should come."

"I'll be here till five in the morning, Kid, you know that." Danny worked all weekend, seemed like.

"Aw, but you can sneak out for forty minutes. It's not far." I handed him two singles I'd earned for mopping up at Fish's and held out my left hand for my change while I stuffed the tip of my pizza into my mouth with my right.

"We'll see," he said with a smirk. "Take care of each other, Kid." And I left, grunting a farewell through my food. It was gone within a block, but it was worth it.

I got moving along Manhattan Avenue again and pulled your pick from my pocket. I squeezed it in my right fist and decided to drop by the comic shop to see Konny.

I don't know what made me decide to do that, really. I knew you wouldn't have been down there; I guess I had half a hope I'd run into you while I walked. It was a long walk, after all, so why not. But I suppose some of me had to reconnect with Konny. I'd hardly seen her this summer, ever since I found you, really. I wondered if she'd take me back—again. Since Jonny's party—seeing Ace—she'd been on my mind a little.

I headed under the BQE and stopped halfway under to enjoy the cool, damp shade of the overpass. The McDonald's called to me, with its siren smell of fries and Mello Yello, but I soldiered on, down Metropolitan to the comic store where Konny had become a fixture. She was behind the counter, leaning on it, playing a GameBoy.

"Where'd you get that?"

Konny shrugged. "Someone left it here last week. Never came back for it."

"You gonna sell it?" I went over to new indies and started flipping through. I didn't really know what I was looking at, though. I was never the comic head Konny was.

"Shit." She flicked the GameBoy off and tossed it onto the couch behind the counter. "Yeah, I guess I will. I hate it anyway."

I started in on the back issues, and Konny came up next to me. "So, what are you doing here?"

I shrugged. "Just wanted to say hi. I haven't seen you in a while." Konny looked at me sideways then dropped onto the couch and flicked the GameBoy back on.

"I can't stop with this thing." It started beeping away.

"So, Fish is letting us play a show at her bar tonight," I said. I pulled an old *Teenage Mutant Ninja Turtles* from its plastic and started flipping through it.

"Fuck," Konny said. "Screw this thing." She slammed the GameBoy down onto the couch beside her. "How is she doing that? I thought she wouldn't let you play as long as you're underage."

"Sixteen-and-over night tonight," I said. I slipped the comic back into its plastic, but Konny jumped up and snatched it away to do it properly. "I mean, if I can find Scout."

Konny laughed and flipped through the back issues to find the comic's rightful spot.

"What?" I said. "Why are you laughing?"

She shook her head and went back to the couch, grabbing up a copy of Wizard from the counter. "Now I know why you're here."

"What's that mean?"

"Two possibilities," Konny said, not looking up from her magazine. "One, you don't know where Scout is, and you're hoping I do."

"Please," I said. "Why would Scout come to a comic shop?"

"Or two," Konny went on, "you're afraid Scout's not coming back, and now you're warming up to me again."

"Fuck you, Konny."

"Ha!" she said. "Number two it is, just like last summer."

"It isn't like that," I insisted. "I just . . . I miss you."

"Of course you do."

Konny's crooked smile stretched just a little, and I knew it was fake—put on to protect her and hurt me. My eyes burned a little, thinking about me and Konny and of me and Felix, and I strode over to the spinning rack of *Archies* and *Betty & Veronica*s before I started crying, and I grabbed hold of it, then pulled it down.

"Are you crazy?" she shrieked at me, jumping up, and yeah, of course I was, because here I was, a year older, and I'd done it again: I'd fallen in love and set myself up to collapse.

I ignored her, though, and walked through the wide-open door of the shop.

At the corner I heard her screaming behind me: "Kid, wait. Come back!"

But I didn't.

THE LOVEBIRDS OF NORTH BROOKLYN

Williamsburg was madness. I guess it always is, but I couldn't handle it—I pulled your guitar pick out of my pocket again and fingered it like a stress stone. The bars along Bedford were already filling up with hipsters while brunch was still being fired for the haute set down the street. A guerrilla garden in a vacant lot near North 5th was swaying gently, and I ran my hand across its fence as I entered the full fray closer to North 7th. Strollers cruised that part of Bedford, sometimes two or three wide, and I took refuge in the gutter, or balanced on the curb—arms out, refusing to act my age—as I walked. But I got bumped once—hard—before I'd even hit the next corner and that was enough. I ducked into the video store, thinking you might be hanging around, sitting on the stool like you do, watching whatever gore or eighties flick they had on the display TVs. It was the only place I could really think to find you. And I thought I knew you so well.

I hated going in there without you. I don't know a thing about film, and the lights are always so low, and there are cases everywhere. Every time I walk in, while my eyes adjust and I feel like I might fall over, I know everyone already inside is watching me, and it's like my first time.

No. Not the first time. The first time was bliss. You led me in and had my hand the whole time, as I met Lill and watched the little TV over the counter with you. You walked me through the selection—by director, because that's how real film people think about film—telling me your favorites (it's not a strong enough word, I know), and as the dim light revealed more and more in your face, I began to see the sparkle in your eyes as you spoke. I began to see where your eyes were going when they were bright like that, because that day, you told me.

But this morning, you weren't there to lead me. I stood just inside the door until I felt steady, then went up to the counter, letting my finger slide over the display on my left to make sure nothing moved. The glass of the counter was cold. I laid one hand flat on it as the boom of a timpani came out of the TV hanging overhead. With my other hand, I squeezed your guitar pick, and on the TV screen a girl with dark hair and eyes like the moon was in the backseat of a car. Rain flowed over the window as she watched another girl running through woods.

"*Suspiria.*" It was Lill. She was sitting on the high stool in the corner. "It's got everything. Brilliant soundtrack. Use of color that will blow your mind." She leaned down a bit and narrowed her eyes at me. "Witches."

I drummed my fingers on the counter and watched the screen, feigned interest for a second. "Has Scout been in this morning?"

"Sorry, Kid," Lill said. She slid a piece of red licorice between her lips, then bit off an inch or so. "Anything important?"

I kept my eyes on the screen. Lill is beautiful and I don't like to look at her for too long, especially while she chews. You know—she's deadly, or something. "We have a gig tonight," I said. "Over at Fish's place."

"On Franklin?" Lill said. I nodded. "Cool. Do you have any flyers for me to give out?"

I shook my head. "It was really last-minute. But listen, tell Scout I was here, okay?" I found my way to the door as Lill said, "Yup."

With one hand on the door, I turned back and watched Lill for a moment, the lights of that movie flickering over her face. Her lips hung just a fraction of an inch apart, and her dark eyes widened as a scream came from the TV. She smirked a little and, without taking her eyes off the screen, said, "What's on your mind, Kid?"

I let go of the door and took a few steps back toward the counter. She held out a licorice whip for me and I took it. After a small bite, I said, "You've spent a little time with Scout, right?"

Lill nodded, still without facing me. On the TV, a blind man walked through an empty European-looking plaza at night. Lill was right: the music was haunting.

"You two have watched a lot of movies together in here, right?"

Lill nodded again, slowly. "Sure, what else?" she said.

"I know you don't know me very well," I said, running a finger along the aluminum trim of the glass countertop. "But does Scout . . . love me?"

Lill finally looked at me. She ignored the screen as the blind man's guide dog suddenly turned on him, tearing into his throat, and she looked at me and laughed, shaking her head.

"It's not funny," I snapped and turned away from Lill's laughing dimples and pointing chin. I blinked hard and forced my eyes to stay on the movie.

She lunged at me and set her fingernails into my upper arm. "Of course it's funny, sweetheart," she said. "Because the love between you two is so obvious it crackles."

I glared at her so she'd go on.

"You two are the lovebirds of north Brooklyn." She pulled a fresh licorice from the cellophane bag in front of her and took a bite, again shaking her head, then looked back at the screen.

. . .

The sun was dropping fast when I left the video store. I blinked and shaded my eyes as I started west from Bedford, but too late. A stocky guy knocked into me and I backed against a tree. He didn't apologize; he hardly looked at me. He just kept talking into his cell phone, ignoring even his girlfriend, covered in boutique and Clinique and not at all unique. I watched them stop in front of a Japanese restaurant, and I slid down the trunk, let myself sit.

I pulled my knees up and folded my arms over them, and I put down my head. I wasn't crying, but I admit I wanted to. Brooklyn was my home, and I loved it—I always had—but my heart had grown, and filling it now was Brooklyn and you. With summer ending, you could be gone—could have been already—and with my heart this big, Brooklyn didn't stand a chance of filling it up without you. I squeezed the pick in my hand tightly, like I could hold on to you.

I lifted my head and leaned on a car parked at the curb to get back to my feet. It was a tiny sports car—forest green. I didn't know if it was the same one I'd seen at the warehouse. It probably wasn't. But I wanted to find nothing but you, and instead I remembered the one person who was your opposite. If I couldn't find you by will alone—by walking from Greenpoint Avenue to Rockaway Beach—I could still do something that would make it possible to move on, to finally give myself to you.

LITTLE SPORTY THING

"Detective Blank," I said as I ran into the station. Behind the high booking desk, a few uniformed cops stopped their conversation to look at me. Behind them, Detective Blank said something quietly into his cell phone, his eyes on me, then slid the phone into his pocket.

"Ms. Weinberg is at your apartment right now," he said. "That was her on the phone."

"I didn't do it," I said, grabbing hold of your hand. "I didn't burn down the warehouse, and I can prove it."

"Yes, you did," he replied, looking away. He found a sheet of paper on the desk and went on as he read it. "Konstantyna Zawadzki, alibi the first. She remembers the night in question—barely, as she was as drunk as you were—but can't be sure of what time the two of you parted ways at McCarren Park, if that is indeed where you parted ways; she wasn't sure."

He put the paper down and found another one in the folder lying open on the desk. "And Anthony Esposito—who you called Ace."

"I didn't know his real name," I said. "Not until just now."

"Well, he was a little slow to tell me anything," the detective went on. "But he wouldn't say for certain that you were even with Zawadzki—"

"Konny"

"—that night. Your alibi is still wide open, Kid. As far as I'm concerned, you're our best shot at wrapping this up. It's not like you're going to jail, Kid. Why the sudden appeal for your innocence?"

I shook my head to clear it, to clear the air of the nonsense the detective had filled it with. "It doesn't matter," I said. "None of that matters. Because there's a lot I haven't told you: I know who did it."

He put both hands on the desk and looked down at me, eyebrows up, waiting.

"Look," I said quickly, glancing at my ragged wet shoes and jamming my hands into my pockets. "I don't know for sure who actually lit the match. But I do know who's responsible."

Blank looked at the other well-dressed cop, then back at me. "Why don't you just tell us what the hell you're talking about."

So I did. I told them all about that little meeting Felix and I had with waterfront development, with the little fat toddler in the ugly expensive clothes, and I told them about that money Felix had been in love with.

"That was last summer?" Blank asked, and I nodded. "Why did the warehouse go down in May, then, almost a year later?"

"I don't know," I said. "He obviously put the assignment on every dreg he could find: me, Felix, the CPM—"

Blank's face went a little softer when I mentioned Felix's name, but he cut me off at CPM.

"CPM?"

"Sorry," I said, hurrying along and stumbling on my tongue a little. "Crazy Polish Man. He lived in the warehouse, and this real-estate guy definitely approached him too."

"How do you know?"

I narrowed my eyes at him and let my thumb roll over the wheel of the lighter in my pocket—even if I wasn't going to smoke, that felt nice. "I don't think I want to get anyone else in trouble," I said. "Just the real-estate guy. He's responsible."

"Kid, we'll decide what matters and who's responsible," Blank said, "and who to arrest on this, okay? What you're saying makes a lot of sense, and we're going to follow every lead we get. But if you're leaving anything out, it's in your best interest to tell us what."

I ran my finger over the wheel of my lighter, spun it safely, knowing the child-proof lighter wouldn't flame even a little. "The crazy man did a lot of . . . ranting," I explained. "Often about the giant toddler. I used to think he meant me."

"You have a young face," Blank said.

"Hence the name," I said, waving him off, "but he didn't mean me. That's what I figured out just now when I thought about the real-estate guy again. His fat face, his thin hair, his scrunched up tantrumy face—he must have given the CPM a real scream one time, so that's how he knows him: giant toddler."

Blank sighed, and I could smell how much coffee he'd had that day. He and the other cop exchanged a look, but I couldn't tell if it meant *We're on to something*, or *This kid's spewing nonsense*. "Did this real-estate guy tell you his name?"

I thought an instant and said no. "I didn't think to ask. And Felix—his eyes were stars for the guy's money. And his car."

"His car?" the other cop said. "It was nice?"

I shrugged. "I don't know from cars," I said. "It was green—and British, Felix said. I think. Looked old, but nice. You know?"

"A coupe? Little sporty thing?"

I nodded. "I guess. Tiny, anyway."

"That's got to be Mausser," he said, looking at Blank. "He owns three of those new condo buildings way down on Kent."

Blank gave him a glance and a smirk.

"What?" the cop said. "I like cars."

Blank tapped the desk with his palm a few times.

"It makes a lot of sense, Detective," the other cop went on. "Listen . . ." His voice quieted a little, just hushed enough so I could hear, but so I'd know I shouldn't be listening. I listened even closer. "Kid didn't do this. The whole warehouse was burning by the time the engines arrived, right? This wasn't a drunken accident by some heartbroken street kid. Let's get Kid's statement and move on this."

But Blank wasn't convinced. "For all we know, you're the one who took Mausser up on this offer. We know you heard the offer; you told us as much," he asked. "What I'm saying, Kid, is why didn't you mention any of this before?"

Could I tell him the truth? Could I tell him I wanted them to pin it on me? That I wished I'd done it, for myself, for you, for Felix. Could I tell them I'd wanted to take the rap, to take the punishment, to put my real guilt to rest? I ran the back of my fist across my lips and shrugged. "I didn't think of it."

The detective sighed.

Back to the other cop, he said, "You're going to tell me that one of the most prominent real-estate developers in Brooklyn went out there and hired a bum to burn down this warehouse?"

"It's a landmark," the other cop said. "He wouldn't have had a choice if he wanted to move quickly on some development down there. And believe me, he wanted to."

"Okay, let's say it's true," Blank said. "Why isn't there a millionaire CPM running around Greenpoint right now?"

That got me. I actually laughed right in Blank's face. "You're as crazy as Felix," I said. "He thought Mausser would actually pay up too."

The other cop smiled at me. "Honestly, Detective," he said. "You don't think a businessman is honoring handshakes with schizophrenic street people, do you?"

Blank stood there, staring at me, for a long moment. Finally he said, "All right, have a seat a minute." He nodded toward the long wooden bench at the wall behind me. It looked like someone had picked up a pew cheap at a church-closing sale. Then Blank and the other cop went into the back again.

I went and took a seat. There were no prostitutes waiting there with me, no old men muttering in a drunken haze, about to be checked into the tank to sleep it off. There were no young black men glaring at me or at the cops. There was just me, sitting at one end of the bench, so I slid down as far as I could go, shoved my hands into my jeans pockets, and watched the industrial, schoolroom clock as the skinny red hand purred around toward out of time.

. . .

For once I had a clock to stare at, and I didn't like it. I traced every minute and every second on that big white-faced clock, its red second hand not ticktocking like it ought to have. It swept around the face, smoothly and confidently. It never faltered, never took a step back, not even for an instant. It didn't skip or change speed. It just ran along in that one-minute circle, over and over. It made me miss the dark cellar, in the middle of the night, when you and I didn't know if it was dinnertime or almost breakfast, so we ate whatever we wanted and drank another Coke each and worked on another song.

. . .

When Detective Blank came in from the back, I was lying on my side along the wooden bench. My neck was stiff and my right arm numb. Night had moved in completely, and I'd hardly taken my eyes off that clock. I heard the bass of boys' car stereos, cruising up and down Greenpoint Avenue, or across Franklin, and their voices calling to each other, in Spanish and Polish. Over them, smoother and more comfortable, I heard joking and mumbling and barking from the cops—right in the room with me, behind the big desk, from rooms off the main one.

"Okay, Kid," Blank said to me. I swung my legs around and sat up. "You can get out of here. You've been helpful."

"I'm off the hook?" I said. The pleading in my voice, and the relief, surprised even me. Didn't I want this rap not twenty-four hours ago? What made me love freedom so much, forgive myself finally for one life and one death? But I knew. I knew it was you.

Blank nodded, only slightly, and said, "Go home, all right?"

I shook my head. "Can't. We have a gig tonight, down at Fish's."

He laughed quickly. "Of course. You play drums, right?"

"Yup."

"I have a cousin plays drums. I'll introduce you." He started for the back, and I called after him.

"Will you come see us play tonight?" I couldn't believe I was inviting the man who arrested me to our gig, especially since I wasn't sure I'd even find you. It seemed now like I wouldn't. Still.

"I'll try to swing by," he said, which meant he wouldn't. I guess the division between those who maintain society and those who try to break it down has to stay firm sometimes. "You tell Fish to card everyone tonight, okay?"

"I will. Gotta go."

I didn't care if he was dismissive. I didn't care if he wasn't the sympathetic civil servant I expected or thought I deserved. I didn't care if I never saw his square mug again. Beaming like the light in your eyes, I jumped up from my police station pew and pushed through the front door.

. . .

My damp sneakers slapped the pavement as I ran, like they had more than a year before when I ran to the warehouse, desperate for another night inside even as it burned. I ran past silent brownstones and a solitary dog walker. She looked at me from under heavy eyelids and tired bangs, stepped back, and yanked the leash as her little dog yapped and thought about my ankles. I turned the corner from Meserole to Franklin hard, right across Calyer and Quay, away from the burned-out warehouse, my body taking an angle like the sidewalk was banked.

Franklin was full, and cheery drunken voices flowed over me—not sentences, not even a clear word. Two men at the corner of Franklin and Greenpoint, outside the Polish club for a cigarette—only feet from where me and Konny first saw Jonny—looked me up and down and wondered: *Chłopak albo dziewczyna?* I gritted my teeth and closed my hands into fists, wishing one of those fists was wrapped around your warm hand.

There were a few more drunks lingering outside at Fish's place. None of them was alone; they were all embracing or touching, holding hands or kissing. They were happy and so alive, even as they slumped or swaggered with weariness or liquor, and I wondered if I'd ever see you again.

GO DOWNSTAIRS

I tore into Fish's place at 11:30. I was hot and tired, and mostly by then I was glad I hadn't found you: my arms and feet and mind weren't ready to drum, my heart was aching, and my eyes were sore and watery, itching from the smoke and grit of a day walking through the last summer sun in Brooklyn. The last thing I wanted to do just then was take the stage behind Felix's kit. I stood by the door—by Valentino, who nodded and smiled at me—and looked the place over, caught my breath.

Inside Fish's wasn't crowded; sixteen-plus nights are always weak. A couple of neighborhood girls were at the bar, hanging on Fish. Ace and his new girl were down at the far end, near the jukebox, watching Jonny hotdog around on the quarters pool table. I noticed the drum set was already upstairs and wondered for a minute who'd set it up, figuring on Jonny or Fish, knowing how worried they get about me—knowing they probably wanted summer to end well for me this year.

"Kid." Dazed, I slowly turned my head to the bar. Fish was leaning across it, holding out a Coke. I walked over and took it. "I was afraid you wouldn't make it," she said.

"I didn't make it. Scout's not here."

Fish smiled at me. "Drink that Coke, Kid. You look about to keel over."

I glanced at Valentino, who looked back at me through those tinted glasses and tidy dreads, and took the straw between my lips. It went down like a treat.

Valentino leaned down from his stool. "Kid," he said. "Go downstairs."

I looked back at Fish, absently handed her the drained, wet glass; it nearly slipped from my hand. "Scout's here?"

Fish smiled when she said, "Scout's not going to leave you, sweetie. Not for long."

I bolted through the bar, even past Jonny, who flashed me his grin and shouted my name, and past the new girl and Ace, who'd moved to the pool table and looked about to screw, out into the back garden. A few customers were out there, hanging around the back fence, smoking cigarettes and nursing cans of PBR and bottles of High Life, but I spun on my heel and hopped down the steps through the garden door into the practice space.

It was dark and quiet, with only Felix's Christmas lights on. I stepped carefully inside and stopped, unwilling to take another step.

(HOW I FOUND FELIX AND LOST HIM)

It was a Sunday night last summer; it was my last night to pretend the summer was magic, to pretend I wouldn't make my way to school in the morning, looking like I'd spent a month living in the gutter. But I couldn't stop pretending, not yet, not with Felix playing a solo set up at Fish's bar, as if to let me have one more night. The crowd was light, but I was there, right up in front. I kept my eyes closed and swayed back and forth with each word—gravel and grit and smoke and smack in every one. Felix's eyes were closed too, because he always sang like that. He wanted to feel alone, he said. "At the end of the day, when everything is over: that's the drone of silence and the ocean and the deep blue, you know?" he would say. "When everything else turns off, when not even a light bulb is humming, when not even a subway is running up in the Bronx, when LaGuardia and JFK shut down, when the cabs don't run and when the Sound and Harbor and ocean all freeze up . . . that's what I'm singing, Kid. That's what I'm praying for every time I close my eyes."

He finished his set and put down the guitar, then just sat on his stool, his eyes closed. He was serene, but not there—he wasn't at Fish's anymore. Still, I clapped and cheered and wanted to grab him, but Jonny held my wrist and took me to the bar and put me on a stool. He ordered me a drink, and Fish looked at him, squarely. But he nodded and she brought me a vodka cranberry that she wouldn't even let Jonny pay for. I sipped it, watching Felix all the while. When the drink was gone, I put my head on the bar so I could still see him, and, listening to Fish and her barback case up empties and kick out drunks, I let myself drift off.

. . .

Jonny woke me up. "It's late, Kid."

"It's almost five, sweetie," Fish said.

I grunted and opened my eyes. There was Jonny. He glanced at Fish, then took my elbow and I got down from my stool.

"My bag," I said. "Downstairs."

"Go through the back," Fish said. "I think the garden door is open."

I started coming to a little stronger once I was on my feet. The stage was empty. "Where's Felix?"

"He left an hour ago," Jonny said. "He was pretty messed up, though, Kid. You didn't need to see that."

"What did he take?"

Fish shrugged and zipped her cash bag. "I need to lock up this shit hole. Run and get your bag, sweetie. Jonny and me will wait for you."

I hobbled past the pool table and the stage, out into the back garden. It was all lit up, in flashing reds and greens and blues and yellows, from the Christmas lights still on and flickering through the wide-open garden door.

"Felix?" I said, stepping down into the dank practice space. It smelled of smoke and sweat and beer and mildew, like it always did, but there was a new smell too. My eyes adjusted quickly to the holiday lighting and I found the couch. Felix was lying there, with his arm out over the side and his feet on the arm of the couch.

"Felix," I said again. "Wake up. I was afraid I wouldn't see you again." But he didn't wake up. So I moved closer to him and took his hand and looked him in the face. His neck was bent so his head craned back, like he'd been straining to see something over the side of the couch. His mouth was twisted a little, half open, like a stroke victim's. But I didn't get it, not yet. I didn't get it until I saw his eyes, sparkling under the colored lights, flashing on and off, red and yellow, green and blue, red and blue, green and yellow. Then I knew he'd found the silence he wanted, with his eyes wide open.

HURRY

I was crying. My chest heaved and I gasped for air down in the dank of the cellar. With every gasp, my shoulders buckled, and I let myself fall backward so my butt was on the top step.

"Kid, what is it?" You came out of the darkness and wrapped yourself around me.

I took a deep breath against your chest. "I can't believe you're here."

"Where else would I be?"

I pulled away and found your eyes, open so wide and beautiful, because they always are, and I couldn't imagine why I'd doubted it.

"How did you find out about the gig?"

You laughed, so I laughed through my hiccups and tears and ran my finger down your forehead and your nose and across your cheek, and pushed your hair behind your ear.

"I didn't find out. I just came down here to find you. Fish told me about it like ten minutes ago."

I took your hand in both of mine. "Where were you all day?"

"After," you said. "Let's go play."

. . .

Fish brought me another perfect Coke after I'd settled in behind the set. I warmed up a bit while you tuned and hiked up your pants twice, three times, and tightened your belt a little. Something white and paper was sticking out of your pocket.

You went up to the mic, and I thought you were sexy as hell. "We're People. I'm Scout. Kid is going to play drums."

We gave them everything, the few people who stood watching, all of them entranced by you like I've always been. Jonny loved you head to toe, but between songs, when I got up and took a towel from Fish, Jonny smiled at me too. Between songs, you turned to me and counted off: *one, two, three, four!* and I thought Ace and the new girl, from the way they leaned on each other and gazed at us, might try to take us both home. Danny came in halfway through the set—did you see?—and smiled at me between songs. Konny was there, and even her boss and landlord Zeph, both beaming.

But best of all, you were there, and when I left the stage so you could be up there alone, and so your dirty-honey voice could roll over me, I held your eyes, and you held mine, and everyone in Fish's bar knew that we were for each other, even if only tonight.

. . .

When it was over, I hopped back onto the stage to break down the set as you hopped down to fall into Jonny's admiring arms. I watched them all, hugging you and kissing your cheeks, tugging at your arm. Everyone knew your secret now, the one I'd had for seventy-four days. I kept my head down and collapsed stands and stacked tom on snare on floor tom.

When I looked back up, the buzzing tiny crowd was without you. My eyes found Konny's, and I pushed toward her and grabbed her hand. She smiled at me.

"I'm sorry," I said.

She kissed my cheek and said, "It's love. I get it."

I smiled up at her, so strong and beautiful, and remembered I loved her first. It wasn't a desperate love, or a dangerous love, and I promised myself I'd hold on to her. Not right then, though. Right then Jonny was between us.

"Kid, I can't believe it." His grin was bigger than ever, and I let myself fall against his chest. His arms collapsed around me.

"Isn't Scout amazing?" I said into his shoulder.

"*You're* amazing," he said. "You're both amazing."

Jonny let me go and shook his head, still smiling, and I grabbed an armful of cymbal stands to bring down to the practice space, out through the back door, into the steady yellow-white light of the naked hanging bulb shining through the wide-open garden door.

"Scout."

You were standing in the center of the room, facing the steps up to the sidewalk out front. Without turning around you said, "Hi, Kid," and I could tell you were smiling.

I leaned the stands against the wall. "You were amazing tonight," I said, coming up behind you. I put my arms around your waist and rested my head on your shoulder. The smell of your day was all over you, and I took a long breath off your neck. We stood like that for a while. "I looked for you today. All day."

"I know. I didn't want to be found."

My chest thumped an extra beat once, then twice, and I held my breath after asking, "Why?"

You didn't respond right away and I lifted my head and moved away from you. I kept my eyes down as I sat on the couch and let myself fall over onto my side to curl up.

"You're leaving," I said to the back of the couch. "Summer is over, and you're leaving."

I felt the couch shift as you sat on its arm, and I felt your hand on my foot, and I felt a chill when you finally spoke. "I was working."

"Working where?" I asked, risking a glance at you, but the security light in the back garden cast a halo over you, and I couldn't see your face. "Doing what?"

You shrugged. "There are some things I know how to do."

"Scout . . ." I sat up. "Tell me what you were doing."

You stared at me, and I hated it. Your eyes, for all the power they hold, could take me to the sunrise and the sunset, across night and day, all across the universe and back. But then they bored into me, leaving me tattered and guilty and ashamed.

You spared me, though, and your eyes went soft again. "I'm not Jonny."

"I know you're not Jonny," I said, dropping my chin.

"I'm not Felix, either."

I went to the back door and just stood there a second looking out. A few kids were still hanging around at Fish's tables. I wanted a cigarette for an instant, so I fiddled with my sticks and turned around. You were inches from me then. "I lost Felix. . . ."

My hands were shaking and tears were starting, so I couldn't look in your eyes. You took my sticks and tossed them onto the couch, then put a hand on my face.

Somehow I raised my chin and you moved closer, and I felt the heat of your breath on my face before your lips finally touched mine, so gently.

When it was over, you answered me. "I was singing."

"Singing?" It hurt a little that you'd sung when I wasn't around to hear it, to bask in it. You nodded and let your hands fall to my waist. I leaned forward so my cheek was against yours and I could smell your hair.

"I went into Manhattan before you woke up. I walked over to Long Island City, up to the 59th Street Bridge, and across to Times Square. I found a corner and just started singing. People stopped, Kid. They stopped and watched me, just me—no band, no guitar. They liked me. They didn't know who I was, or where I'd come from, but when I sang, they liked me, and they gave me money. A cop watched for one song, and he gave me a buck, but then he told me to beat it. But I didn't mind. I set up again, and then again, at different corners in different parts of town. I needed a lot of money. I needed it for you."

"For me?"

You pulled away from me and I felt cold, but you reached into your back pocket and pulled out an envelope. "I needed it for this."

"What is it?" I stared at the envelope, waiting for you to hand it to me, but you just held it and watched my face. I moved closer to you to warm myself again.

"I want to take you to the sunrise, just once before the summer ends."

"We see the sunrise nearly every morning, Scout— since I found you in front of Fish's bar. Don't you remember?"

You shook your head. "No. You haven't seen it properly. You haven't seen the sun rise up from the end of the world."

Finally you handed me the envelope and I tore it open. Two yellow and blue cards were inside. "MetroCards?"

You smiled and said, "We have to hurry."

. . .

I'm not sure when I was asleep and when I was awake. There were subways. There were worried looks from strangers as we switched off sips from our can of Mello Yello, but I stared them down and smiled. *We're in love*, I thought. *You can't hurt us.*

There was the Long Island Rail Road, there was a chill at Jamaica when you led me onto and across the platform, and we kissed before the doors closed. I fell asleep again with my head on your lap. The conductor was young, without a cap on, and you handed over our tickets. I looked up at your face and saw pride there, and felt proud myself, because your eyes were right there—open—with me instead of flying off.

And then we walked. It must have been miles, around the Harbor, watched over by a rich-looking hotel from a different time, and through hilly neighborhoods of winding roads and more trees than I'd ever seen, and I was amazed you knew where to go. It was desolate, and if not for the smell and sound of the ocean, we could have been anywhere in the country—except for the city, except for Brooklyn. Still, every turn you had the way memorized and I knew this was your home, so I held your hand and we reached the beach, with its lighthouse and rocky coast, just as the sun was creeping up from the water.

I squeezed your hand and looked at your face. It was lit up, not from the rising sun, but from within, and I knew mine must have been too. We smiled at each other, and without a word ran the last hundred yards to the rocks and the sun, and the constant roar and crash of the Atlantic as it struck the end of the world.

AUTHOR'S NOTE

Although *Brooklyn, Burning* is a work of fiction, it takes place in a real neighborhood and centers on an actual event. Very early on the morning of May 2, 2006, the Greenpoint Terminal Warehouse in Brooklyn caught fire. It burned for days, eventually earning ten alarms and requiring hundreds of firefighters. Investigators suspected foul play. After a month-long investigation, two homeless men were sought for the crime, and police claimed to have a confession from one of them. He later said they misunderstood him, and that he had not confessed. Still denying his guilt, he was sentenced to three years of probation and alcohol rehabilitation. That man has since returned to his native country, Poland.

Meanwhile, skeptical New Yorkers had their eyes on a real-estate developer. Greenpoint, a Brooklyn neighborhood that bordered on the recently hip Williamsburg, looked primed to be the next cool Brooklyn waterfront area. Many cried "scandal," "arson," and even "conspiracy." After all, the warehouse sat on prime real estate, but it was also a historic building and therefore protected. No developer would have ever been able to build towering apartment buildings on the site. With the warehouse a burned-out shell, though, it was suddenly possible. The investigation became headline news. Although the case is still open when *Brooklyn, Burning* ends, in reality it is very closed, having been ruled an accidental fire started by a homeless Polish immigrant.

The Greenpoint Terminal Warehouse had been a popular hangout and shelter for homeless people, some of them likely young. The primary reason for youth homelessness is difficulty at home. According to the National Coalition for the Homeless, "more than half of the youth interviewed during shelter stays reported that their parents either told them to leave or knew they were leaving and did not care" (http://www.nationalhomeless .org/factsheets/youth.html). Among homeless youth, LGBTQ youths are disproportionately represented. It's not a great stretch to assume that these kids' sexuality and their parents' inability to accept and approve is the core of the problem. To help, or if you need help, visit nationalhomeless.org.

Beyond that, the geography of Greenpoint is as accurate as I could make it, using my own memories of the place when I lived there—and a little help from good old Google Maps. Several real businesses are alluded to or even mentioned by name, but—to my knowledge—there has never been a bar on Franklin run by a woman called Fish. The Pencil Factory, Jonny's other favorite watering hole, does exist. It's a very nice bar, and they were serving excellent grilled sandwiches the last time I was there. They were not, however, serving people under twenty-one. (Sorry, Kid.)

ACKNOWLEDGMENTS

Thanks first, once again, to Andrew and Edward. I think we make a fine literary, musical, and culinary critical trio. Let's do it again soon.

Thanks also to my faraway family: my mother and brother, for so many years of support. And to my Minnesota family: MIL, FIL, and SILs; this book was written almost entirely during your relentless babysitting work.

Thanks to the Loft, for existing, and to my Loft classmates, the first people to read this, before it was probably worth reading. Thanks also to the Minnesota writers whom I've had the pleasure of meeting and sometimes working with over the last couple of years; it's amazing to be part of such a strong and present community of writers, especially writers of literature for young people.

Some of the earliest readers of this book—in its earliest draft: before there was even a fire—were my short-lived online writing group, the Otters: Josh Berk, Jonathan Roth, Kurtis Scaletta, and Jon Skovron. They helped me see that two kids kicking around Brooklyn isn't a story. Thanks for the notes, guys.

Thanks to two other communities, as well—one large, and one small: one, the first generation of Lab Rats, Ilsa J. Bick and Blythe Woolston, and two, the Tenners. How writers ever survived without such support is beyond me.

Finally, thanks to the two wonderful and constantly amazing people I have the pleasure to share a little house with: Beth and Sam. You are my inspiration every single day.

ABOUT THE AUTHOR

Steve Brezenoff is the author of dozens of chapter books for younger readers and the young adult novel *The Absolute Value of -1*. Born in Queens, Steve has lived in the suburbs on Long Island, on a couch on Manhattan's Upper East Side, a few feet from the 7 train in the Sunnyside neighborhood in Queens, and across the Hudson River in Jersey City—but none of those places has stuck with him or been missed as acutely as Brooklyn, where he lived on and off for much of his twenties and early thirties.

Steve left an apartment in Greenpoint, the northernmost Brooklyn neighborhood, when he moved to Minnesota with his dog, Harry (who was rescued from East New York—the tough Brooklyn neighborhood where Steve's father grew up). It was in that apartment that he proposed to his wife, Beth (the reason he moved to Minnesota). If you ask, he'll admit that yes, he hopes, intends, and expects to move back to Brooklyn some day. For now, he lives in St. Paul, with Beth, their son, Sam, and Harry.

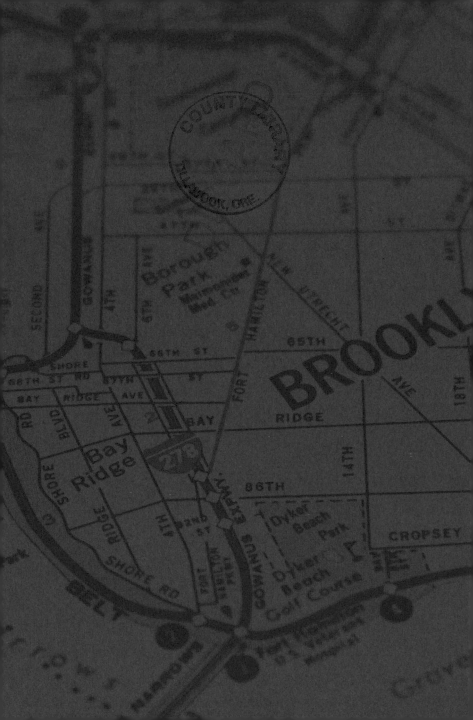